Colby's gaze

It was as if he were s[...]
developed since the [...]
honest with each other.

Anna let her thoughts grow and expand, knew they filled her eyes even as they filled her heart. She was being more open with him at this moment than she had been since his return....

"Would you mind singing it as I play so I can hear the words inside my head?"

Colby's voice seemed to come from a long tunnel, taking its time to reach her brain.

Anna jerked away and turned back to the piano keys. She must guard her heart. And thoughts. Hadn't she learned that lesson already?

So she played. He played. And she sang.

And despite her constant mental warnings, Anna let the music wash over her, numb her caution. She knew a height of pleasure so new and unfamiliar she didn't even know what to call it.

It was the music. That was all. Nothing more...

LINDA FORD

shares her life with her rancher husband, a grown son, a live-in client she provides care for, and a yappy parrot. She and her husband raised a family of fourteen children, ten adopted, providing her with plenty of opportunity to experience God's love and faithfulness. They had their share of adventures, as well. Taking twelve kids in a motorhome on a three-thousand-mile road trip would be high on the list. They live in Alberta, Canada, close enough to the Rockies to admire them every day. She enjoys writing stories that reveal God's wondrous love through the lives of her characters.

Linda enjoys hearing from readers. Contact her at linda@lindaford.org or check out her Web site at www.lindaford.org, where you can also catch her blog, which often carries glimpses of both her writing activities and family life.

LINDA FORD

THE
Cowboy's
Baby

Steeple
Hill®

Published by Steeple Hill Books™

STEEPLE HILL BOOKS

Steeple
Hill®

Recycling programs
for this product may
not exist in your area.

ISBN-13: 978-0-373-82834-0

THE COWBOY'S BABY

Copyright © 2010 by Linda Ford

Printed in U.S.A.

They that trust in the Lord shall be as mount Zion, which cannot be removed, but abideth forever.
—*Psalms* 125:1

I have been blessed by godly teaching from many preachers and teachers. Bill Gurnett and Mr. Fairholme played an important role in my early spiritual development but there are many, many more. I dedicate this book to preachers everywhere who faithfully teach God's word.

Chapter One

Steveville, Dakota Territory
May 1876

The pounding on the door threatened to bring down the roof. Twenty-year-old Anna Caldwell resisted an urge to call for patience as she raced to answer the summons before the racket woke the baby. Nothing made eighteen-month-old Dorrie crankier than having her afternoon nap cut short.

Anna paused long enough to take in a deep breath, lift her head and compose her expression to reveal none of her annoyance. After all, as the preacher's daughter and his housekeeper, she was expected to maintain a high standard of conduct. She pulled open the door and fell back half a step, gasping as her lungs spasmed so tight her chest hurt. "You. What are you doing here?"

Colby Bloxham stood before her, as handsome as ever. No. Even more handsome if that were possible. His dark blond hair fell past his ears, the ends faded by the sun. His blue eyes shone as bright as the sky behind him.

Her eyes stung and her throat burned as she recognized similar features she saw every day in the sweet face of Dorrie—his daughter. He'd left her—abandoned her—to Anna's care. Surely he didn't intend to upset the pleasant arrangement. He wouldn't dare.

He tipped the brim of his hat back with the barest flick of one finger. "Hello."

Anna stiffened her spine. "What do you want?" She kept her voice calm.

Colby's grin widened with confidence that she would welcome him again. His eyes smiled even more beguilingly than his mouth.

She didn't welcome him. She wouldn't. With a coolness she didn't feel, she ran her gaze up and down his length, hoping to convey how unwelcome he was. His grayish-brown trousers and tan shirt were faded in the areas that took more wear but surprisingly clean.

"I've come back."

"Didn't I tell you I never wanted to see you

again?" It had been a year since he'd last entered this house, roaring with the effects of the contents of a bottle he still held, frightening Dorrie into hysterical screaming. It was the last straw as far as Anna was concerned. She'd had her fill of his carousing and having to listen to reports of his drunken behavior. She wanted nothing more than to protect Dorrie from such things. And perhaps shelter her own feelings, as well.

"I've changed."

She sniffed air surprisingly void of the repulsive smell of alcohol. "I can tell you haven't."

"You can help me."

"I've already tried. Several times." Each time her life had ended up more tattered than the last, her emotions shredded. She would not let history be repeated. "Not again."

The words were bravely spoken but forced with difficulty from her mouth. Her heart felt as if it had been rung hard by a strong washerwoman. She shuddered. Could she prevent him causing trouble over Dorrie? She should have gone to the judge and asked for legal adoption but as an unmarried woman, even with evidence of Colby abandoning his child... Well, she likely didn't have much chance of obtaining the necessary documents and she thought she'd never have to worry.

"You always help me."

She closed her eyes to his pleading tones.

"Anna, don't you give up on me. I've got nothing, no one else if you do." His voice rose with every word.

The commotion woke Dorrie and she cried.

"Is that my baby girl?"

"Colby." The feel of his name on her lips filled her with such sweet sorrow.

She swallowed hard and forced herself to speak his name again. "Colby, go away and leave us alone. I don't want to see you." She managed to slam the door and press her back to it. Her knees buckled. She slipped down the length of wood. Delving into her willpower, she stopped her descent and forced determination to her legs. Was he gone? She heard the thud of her heartbeat against her eardrums but no sound of boots marching away.

Go away, Colby. Leave us alone. Leave us in peace.

Dorrie continued to cry and call, "Mama." Anna had taught Dorrie to call her such, thought there would never be any question that she'd be the one to raise Dorrie, be the only mother the baby ever knew.

She never expected Colby to show his face in Steveville again.

For the space of several breaths, Anna could not

move. Only when she heard Colby stomp away did she draw in a full-size breath, sending resolve clear to her toes.

"Mama." What a delightful sound that single word from Dorrie's mouth.

But knowing Colby was back forced Anna to face the truth. She was not Dorrie's mama and could lose the baby at the whim of a man who found courage and comfort from a bottle.

But he wouldn't take the baby without a fight. Anna wasn't much good at dealing with conflict. She'd sooner people just got along. But anyone trying to take Dorrie from her would discover the fury she was capable of.

Colby paused at the bottom of the steps and turned to face the door. "I ain't drunk." He'd made up his mind he wasn't going to be like his old man and drown in his drink. He'd tried that direction and finally got sick of it. Surprised him some, it had taken so long. He got sick of a few other things he'd been and done in the recent months of his life, as well.

He sniffed at his arms. Couldn't smell anything amiss but if Anna did maybe he should have spent more time soaking in the river before he came here.

The baby continued to cry. With a start, he realized she interspersed her cries with words. She could talk. Of course she wouldn't still be a baby. Wonder how big she was now. He couldn't get a picture in his mind of what this child of his would now look like. He had a hard time thinking of her as his child. He'd thrust the infant into Anna's arms shortly after birth and seen little of her since. He had only one memory of Dorrie, two if he counted clutching the newborn and rushing to Anna with her. The one time he recalled through an alcohol-induced haze was of the wide-eyed fear in the baby's face and her piercing screams of terror before Anna managed to shove him out the door ordering him to leave and never return. In hindsight he couldn't say he blamed her, though at the time he'd been plenty angry.

"I'm not going away." His voice echoed in his ears. He intended to be the kind of father to Dorrie he'd always wanted.

And never had.

He refused to believe Anna didn't want to see him. From the day he wandered into Steveville on the tail end of a cattle drive, only sixteen years old and already on his own for two years, he'd found a welcome with Anna that he'd found nowhere else. Not even with his deceased wife. He had married Nora for all the wrong reasons just as she'd married him for equally wrong ones.

He stared at the church to the right of the house,

recalling in brilliant detail how he'd passed the building six years ago and seen fourteen-year-old Anna coming from the interior, beautiful as a western songbird and singing just as sweetly. Right then and there he'd decided he might give church a try.

From the beginning, he felt something special for Anna and she, he was certain, for him. She'd understood him, listened to him, encouraged his dreams and hopes just as he'd listened to hers. Mostly their dreams had been of a good solid home with a loving father and mother and several children. Funny how they shared similar dreams coming from such different backgrounds.

He wondered if she had the same hopes and dreams she'd once had. Or had they died along with the welcome he'd expected?

He continued to stare at the church. He kind of thought God would welcome him back, too. But maybe He didn't want to see Colby Bloxham any more than Anna did. *Go away. I don't want to see you.* The words banged against the inside of his head, filling his thoughts with old familiar feelings of being something from the slop bucket.

He swung up on his horse, his first instinct to ride the animal into a lather, straight down the road and away from all this. But Dorrie's cries continued. His child.

Somehow he would prove to Anna he had changed and could be a father to Dorrie. It was time. 'Course he could try and take Dorrie without her consent. After all, the little girl was his. But he suspected Anna might fight him and no doubt everyone would take her side. Besides, for some reason, it was important to him to win Anna's approval. A large ache carved itself into his heart by the words echoing through his mind. *Go away. I don't want to see you.*

But he was not going anywhere.

He turned to the left, and rode into the main part of town, glancing about as he passed the houses on each side of the dusty street. Things looked much as they had when he left. Somehow he'd expected them to be different. As if his own decision to be different would have changed everything else in his world.

The houses gave way to businesses—the blacksmith and livery barn set back from the street, the sounds of metal on metal ringing through the air, the smell of horses and hay filling his nostrils. The signs on each store were familiar—Mack's Mercantile, the feed store, the milliner, the lawyer. He stopped at the Lucky Lady Saloon and dismounted. His hands on the swinging doors, he hesitated. He'd had enough of drinking and so much more but he had friends he wanted to see.

He pushed the doors aside and strode in.

He avoided looking at the bright patch where the sun filtered through the dirty window as he gave his eyes three seconds to adjust to the dim light. A familiar figure nursed a bottle at the nearest table and he sauntered over. "Hey, Arty." The old codger had wandered into town a year or so after Colby had arrived. Arty had known both Colby and his old man way back when. Colby always wondered that they'd landed in the same place but guess all Arty had to do was follow any road long enough and he was bound to get somewhere even if only Steveville. At first he had resented the old man's presence, reminding him as it did of Pa, but Arty was harmless. He got sloppy drunk not fighting drunk.

"Colby? When did you get back in town? What are you doing with yourself?" Arty jerked toward the bar. "Sol, get us another glass. Colby here is going to share my bottle."

"Don't use that stuff anymore."

Poor old Arty almost jolted off his chair. "You're joshing. A Bloxham that don't drink. Ain't possible."

An old familiar anger at his upbringing seared through Colby like a struck match then died as quickly and harmlessly. "I decided I didn't want to turn out like my old man."

Arty studied the bottle regretfully and yet affectionately. "Wise move, my boy. So watcha been doing?"

He wasn't about to tell anyone the truth about where he'd been and what he'd done since he'd last wandered the streets of Steveville. Hopefully news of his doings hadn't trickled back this far and never would. But Arty waited, clutching his glass with both hands and studying Colby with the unblinking stare of a man whose thought processes had been dulled by drink.

"Arty, I been wandering around a bit."

"Looking for anything in particular?"

Colby laughed. "Yup. Me."

Arty blinked, drained his glass, wiped his mouth and tried to decide whether to laugh or sob.

Colby patted the older man's shoulder. "Never mind. It don't make sense to me, either." He'd glanced around the room when he first entered, noted several men but paid them scant attention. Now he looked around again, hoping to see a familiar face or two. He specially wished to see Hugh, the only man who'd felt like a friend. He used to come over and play cards with Colby and Nora in the evenings and often stayed the night. Hugh had been with him after Nora's death. Colby didn't know how many times Hugh had dragged him from the bar and made sure he got home before he got arrested. Saved his hide on one specific occasion, yet last time he'd seen Hugh, Colby had been fighting drunk and accused the man of all sorts of horrible things. Even accused him of having his eyes on Nora. Some way to treat a friend who had likely saved him from the hangman's noose.

He didn't see Hugh but met the eyes of a bold stranger, recognizing immediately a man itching for trouble.

The man left the bar and moseyed over to flick a finger at Arty's bottle, bringing a defensive grab from the older man. "This old drunk a friend of yours?"

There was a time in the near past when Colby would have jumped at the chance to respond. But no more. He thought of sweet Anna, who had once been his friend, and the way she'd looked at him, ordering him away like some kind of rabid dog. Yeah, she might have once had good reason to think so, but he'd win back her friendship if it took the rest of his life.

He hoped it wouldn't take near that long.

"Let the old man alone," he murmured in a soft, not-wanting-a-fight tone. "He ain't hurting no one."

"He hurts my nose." The dark-eyed stranger chose to flick at Arty's hat, sending it askew.

Arty clung to it with both hands like he feared further tormenting.

Colby pushed his own hat back so the man could see his expression clearly and crossed his arms over his chest. "I said leave him alone."

The man jeered. "Says who?"

Colby recognized the challenge. Hoped he wouldn't have to accept it. He gave the man his hardest look, one birthed before his sixth birthday and matured over the years. This past year had given it a whole new depth. He allowed himself a moment of victory as the annoying man shrugged and returned to his drink at the bar, muttering, "Ah, who cares? Just another old drunk. Seen hundreds of 'em."

Colby pulled his hat back to where it usually rode. Hugh wasn't there. He'd determined that. But he deliberately lingered in the saloon for a while longer, not wanting anyone to think he had reason to hurry away. But he knew if he stayed too long word would somehow get back to Anna about where he chose to spend his time. He knew small towns, knew this one better 'n most. Person couldn't so much as cough without it being reported and discussed freely. He knew her opinion about the evils of drinking. Had heard it many times especially after Dorrie was born. "Won't find any solution in the bottle," she said. He remembered the perverse pleasure he got out of asking her where she thought he'd find an answer for his loss.

Always she said the same thing. *God is the great healer. God has a plan for your life. God loves you.* He almost believed. So many times he almost believed.

But how could God love him when he constantly found himself in one sort of trouble after another. Sure, anyone would say it was of his own making. For the most part, it was. But this time he intended to prove he was something more than a Bloxham living from a bottle. A better Bloxham than his father was or that he'd been in the past.

He waited a suitable amount of time then sauntered out the door as if it mattered not to him if he stayed or left.

He led his horse down the street, his feet aching to wander south toward the church and Anna. He didn't believe she truly meant it when she said she never wanted to see him again, but it might be wisest to give her a chance to get used to him being back in town and adjust to the idea he had changed.

He forced his steps to some of his familiar haunts, thinking he might find Hugh. But after an hour of looking he'd not seen the man. Likely he'd show up after he finished whatever job he currently held. Colby would make a swing by the Lucky Lady again later in the evening.

In the meantime…

Well, he'd give anything to see Anna hurrying

between the house and the church like he had that very first time. Maybe he'd just ride on down the street, casual-like, no hurry, no destination in mind. Might be she'd have cause to cross the yard, perhaps carrying his little daughter with her. He wondered if Dorrie favored him or Nora. Or did she reveal a likeness to both her parents?

Anna carried Dorrie to her high chair. For a moment she held her close and buried her face against Dorrie's warm neck, breathing in the familiar scent. "My sweet, sweet baby." This child filled her with such joy. What if Colby had come back to claim her? Anger and determination drilled through her limbs and up her spine.

She would stand between Dorrie and her father, fight him like a wildcat, protect Dorrie from anything that would hurt her. No matter what. She loved this child as her own.

Dorrie squirmed. "Down, Mama."

Anna reluctantly ended her hug and put the baby in her chair. She'd brushed Dorrie's blond hair back and tied it with a white ribbon, letting little curls escape to frame the heart-shaped face. For the past year, she had allowed herself to pretend Dorrie was hers, allowed herself to believe Colby would never return, a thought that filled her with a strange mixture of relief and regret. She'd never been certain which was the stronger emotion.

Dorrie drank half her milk then threw back her head and wailed.

"Poor baby. You didn't get enough sleep, did you?"

And Colby was to blame. His loud intrusion had woke the baby. What did he want? Why had he returned? Her insides tightened until she wondered if something she'd eaten had been a little off. "Let's go find Poppa." She plucked the child from her chair, wiped her face and settled her on her hip.

"See Poppa?"

"Yes, pet. We'll see your poppa." She hated to disturb Father at the church where he went to meditate but she badly needed his counsel.

She ducked out the back door. The wall of the church was blackened. The sight still gave her heart a jerk. The fire had taken out several homes and damaged the church before it was quenched. Thank God the fire had stopped when it did. Thank God no lives had been lost, though a few families had lost homes.

Guilt weaved throughout her thoughts. She really didn't have time to wander around nursing her worries. Alex would soon be home from school, needing supervision. Supper needed making and she must finish sewing together the quilt top the women were making for the Anderson family who were among those who'd lost their homes. Tomorrow afternoon the sewing circle would gather at the manse to put together the quilt.

But first she would find some peace at the church and at Father's side.

As she crossed the yard she noted a saddled horse on the other side of the road, in the shelter of some trees where the road branched off to a pathway leading to the narrow river cutting past the town. Strange that a horse should be left thus. Then she saw Colby lounging in the shadow of the trees. Did he intend to spy on them, perhaps wait for a chance to snatch his daughter?

She clutched Dorrie tighter and raced into the shelter of the church. "Father," she called, her voice tight with unformed terror, "he's come back. What are we going to do?"

Chapter Two

Colby saw Anna look in his direction, noted how she jerked in surprise and likely a whole lot of anger, then raced into the church. She obviously didn't like the fact he was there. He doubted she wanted to know he intended to stay around. She'd hurried into the church so fast he'd gotten no more than a glimpse—just enough to make him want more. He recalled a time when they had spent many an hour wandering down the nearby path discussing anything and everything and sometimes nothing. It was the only time in his life he'd felt real and honest.

He'd run from that, driven by his own internal demons. But wherever he'd run, whatever he'd done—and he hoped no one would ever know what that was—a vast hollowness sucked at his heart.

Only one thing had ever satisfied that emptiness—Anna's presence.

He'd seen the child perched on Anna's hip. Dorrie. Grown considerably. In the seconds he'd had to study her he could say she looked a sturdy child with hair somewhat fairer than his own with a big white bow in the back. He wanted to see and know this tiny bit of humanity he'd made with Nora. He'd come back to be a proper father but he knew so little about being one except to know he didn't want to be like his pa.

He guessed Anna wouldn't be leaving the sanctuary of the church while he stood there. "I'll be back," he muttered as he swung to Pal's back.

Several hours later he strode into the Lucky Lady and checked the occupants. No sign of Hugh. Was he still around the area or had he left for something better—or at least different? *Could save your energy, Hugh. Different ain't better.*

Arty sat at the same table, his eyes now glassy, his hat askew. Another familiar figure sat across from him—Tobias—neat and tidy as always, and rough shaven just as Colby remembered. He wondered if the man used a dull table knife for a razor.

He saw it all in a glance even as he watched the dark-eyed troublemaker nod to the men on either side of him who then slid away as the man slowly uncoiled himself from the bar to slither toward Colby.

"This the one who caused you a problem?" The question came from Colby's right.

He tensed, feeling as much as seeing, the two crowding close. He kept his attention on the man crossing the room. *Keep coming. Bring your trouble to me. Leave poor old Arty alone.*

But the man stopped and slapped the table in front of Arty. He jumped and half tumbled from his chair.

Colby eased forward prepared to help though he perceived it wasn't Arty the dark-eyed man wanted to tangle with. "Leave him be."

"Who? This old drunk?" He grabbed the bottle from the table and tipped it over. Only a few drops spilled out as Arty had already drained it, but the old man cried out and lurched to rescue it as if it held several generous drinks.

The man pushed Arty aside. "Sit down, old man. Before you end up facedown in the sawdust."

Arty stumbled backward, swayed and clutched at the stranger's arm to steady himself.

"Get away from me, you old bum." The trouble-maker tossed Arty aside.

Colby saw Arty was going to land heavily and he strode forward to catch him.

He didn't make two steps before his arms were

caught on each side. Helplessly he watched Arty skid to the floor and flounder for a grasp on something solid. He found the rung of the chair and started to pull himself back to its seat only to have the chair kicked away from him.

Colby growled. "Leave him alone."

The third man left Arty and marched over to glower into Colby's eyes. "You think you scare me?"

"Enough that you enlist two more the same as you to even the odds." He grunted as the man on his right shoved his arm up his back hard enough to tear at his shoulder. "Just you and me. Let's see how scared you are then."

The man nodded to his friends. But he didn't wait for them to release Colby's arms to sucker punch him in the stomach and, before Colby could get his fists bunched, landed a blow to his nose.

Ignoring the pain and the blood pouring forth, Colby exploded into a fury of fists. He had the man on the floor before the other two grabbed him. They succeeded in dragging him to the door and tossing him out on the street but Colby made them work for their victory.

As he wiped away the blood and scrambled to his feet, several decent folk passed by on the other side bound, no doubt, for some noble event.

"Why, it's Colby Bloxham."

"As rowdy as ever, I see."

A loud sniff and then a pious "Let's pray he leaves again real soon," followed.

Colby grabbed his hat and smacked it hard on his head. He'd give it until morning for Anna to hear that Colby had been brawling. He could explain if she'd give him a chance. 'Course she'd given him many chances in the past and he'd mangled each of them. Not much wonder she wasn't about to throw open the door to welcome him this time.

No point in expecting a chance to explain himself.

He strode away, heading for the camp he'd set up on the edge of town, close enough to the river for ease of water, close enough to the church he could slip over and watch the goings-on, yet not so close as to give anyone cause for concern.

Anna covered the little cakes with clean towels and arranged the fancy teacups on the table. The members of the Ladies Sewing Circle would be arriving any minute. Everything was ready, in precise perfection. She should be calm and serene.

She was not.

Her emotions raged as she filled the kettle. Father had said it was only natural for Colby to want to see how Dorrie was faring. And perhaps he had truly changed. They needed to encourage him in that direction. After all, hadn't they often prayed he would turn to God to meet the needs of his heart?

Anna couldn't meet Father's eyes as he spoke. Some time ago her prayers had shifted from asking for Colby's redemption to asking that he never return. How would she survive having her heart ripped out and left to whimper and bleed again? And now the threat was twofold. She could also lose Dorrie. She'd said so to Father.

"Did he say he wanted to take her?"

"He asked to see her."

"Natural enough, as I said. Let's leave it in God's loving care." He'd taken her hand in his and prayed.

But Anna didn't find the peace and release she'd hoped for. She couldn't stop wondering what Colby really wanted. She couldn't stop worrying how his plans could upset her life.

Her teeth ached from continually fighting this inner battle and she forced her jaw to relax. *Please, God, put Your mighty hand on his back and send him down the road again.*

Such an ache consumed her that she bent over and moaned. *Anna, forget the boy you once knew. Colby is no longer that person. Let him go.*

Forcing herself to concentrate on the task at

hand, she filled the cream and sugar then paused to run a hand over her hair, making sure every strand was in place. She'd changed earlier and the white shirtwaist was immaculate as was the black skirt she'd brushed thoroughly. No one could find fault with her appearance.

But if they could see the turmoil of her heart they might have cause to wonder about her suitability to run the pastor's home.

She pulled herself taller. She needed to trust God. She said the words. She meant them. But she still felt no peace. Would God allow her to experience loss once again? Pain shafted through her, consuming her. Then she pulled her self-control tight as a corset. Whatever lessons God wanted to teach her through her sorrows, she had tried to learn them. She didn't want the lesson repeated.

Lord, I try to be obedient and do what You would want.

That's what she needed to concentrate on—trusting and being obedient.

She hurried into the other room where she had pushed back the wooden armchair and moved the little side table to make room to set up the quilting frame. The top was finished and waiting. The ladies had each contributed to the squares for the quilt. Today they would assemble it with batting and backing and tie it. Anna would finish the edging and then present it to the Anderson family, who had lost everything in the fire.

"It's a mercy no one was killed," Mrs. Klein said later as the ladies worked on the quilt. The fire still filled their thoughts and conversation.

"God be praised," Mrs. Berglund said.

"Now we must do our part to help those who lost their home. Thank God we can make this quilt."

"God be praised," Mrs. Berglund said.

Anna bent over the quilt, hiding a smile. Mrs. Berglund was a dear soul but so predictable, her comments invariably limited to one or two of her favorite phrases.

"I thought Mrs. Anderson might enjoy helping us with the quilt. Did you ask her to attend?" Mrs. Percy directed her question at Anna.

"I did invite her but she is struggling to cope in the little shack they're living in. I don't think she feels up to visiting just yet." Mrs. Anderson had fluttered her hands and looked about wildly when Anna had gone to visit. Anna couldn't imagine losing everything and trying to live in a building that hadn't been intended for human habitation.

"Some of us gathered for tea last night." Mrs. Percy sat up and looked around at her announcement. She waited until she had everyone's attention before she continued. "Now that everyone is safely sheltered and resuming their lives, it's high time, I say, to get the church fixed up so we can meet there." She sniffed. "I've never cared for taking my children to that room above the saloon."

Anna said nothing as the other women murmured their comments. Certainly it wasn't ideal, but helping the people who lost their homes and belongings took precedence over fixing the church. She waited, knowing Mrs. Percy had more to say on the subject now that all eyes were on her.

"Pastor Caldwell said he'd look after the repairs but I've seen no evidence of it getting done." She cleared her throat and gave Anna a hard look, driving Anna's heart to the bottom of her stomach in alarm.

"Remember we agreed to be part of the town's celebration in honor of Mr. Steves. It's imperative the repairs are done in time. After all, Mr. Steves donated the money for building the church. We need to remember him for that."

Anna felt every pair of eyes turn toward her. Though no one spoke she knew what they were all thinking—the same thing as she. Father's intentions were good but every one jabbing their needles into the quilt knew he tended to get lost in his thoughts and forget such practical things as filling the stove, or closing a window. She couldn't imagine he would keep his mind on the mundane things such as carpentry and painting long enough to see the task completed in time for the big seventy-fifth birthday party planned for the town's founder. Why had he agreed to be in charge?

She sat up straight and met each pair of eyes around the quilt, smiling serenely and reassuringly. "I think you can count on Father to get it done in time." She'd personally see that he did. She'd remind him to arrange the workers needed. Father was a godly man and his concern for others was genuine but he needed help with practical matters. She would provide that help, gently and discreetly, not only because it was her duty as her father's unofficial assistant as running his household turned out to be, but also because it was plain if the repairs weren't done she would be found wanting in the eyes of the women seated in her front room.

The others murmured approval and returned to their sewing.

"Mama, Mama, Mama," Dorrie called.

"Excuse me. I have to get her up from her nap." Anna hurried to the little girl. Having Colby show up stole from her bliss in having a child she considered her own without benefit of marriage nor condemnation of a child born out of wedlock. *Please, God. Send that man on his way. I don't want Dorrie hurt by the things he does.* She knew people would find it easy to blame every naughty thing Dorrie did as evidence she was living up to her heritage. Or rather, down to it. Anna could well imagine Mrs. Percy sniffing and saying, "An apple doesn't fall far from the tree."

Although Dorrie wasn't the only one who could be hurt, she was young and might easily forget Colby wandering into her life and out again.

Anna doubted she would recover as quickly.

She slipped a clean white pinafore over Dorrie's blue dress and put on her shoes. "There you go. All pretty. Remember the ladies are here so I want you to say hello to them all and then play quietly." Anna took from the shelf the Noah's Ark and animals reserved for times when Dorrie had to play quietly at her side.

She returned to the front room and the sewing circle.

Mrs. Percy oohed over Dorrie a minute then turned her sharp gaze toward Anna. "I saw her father last night."

Anna's heart dropped to the soles of her feet. Whatever the woman intended to say had the potential to upset Anna's world.

"In the most shameful state of being tossed from that horrible saloon. I'm not much to pay attention to rumors—"

Anna steeled her expression to remain kind and

calm, displaying none of the disbelief she felt at the woman's assurances, nor her fear of what more would follow.

Mrs. Percy continued. "But it seems whenever I hear the name Colby Bloxham it comes in the same sentence as robbery, plunder or other illegal activity." She sniffed and pasted on a pitying expression. "I wouldn't be surprised to see a wanted poster with his likeness on it."

Anna wanted to cry out a protest. But why should she want to defend him? The man had gone from bad to worse. Her only concern was to protect Dorrie from the ugliness of such speculation.

Thankfully, Dorrie was too young for the discussion to affect her. But how long before the unkind words would sear her little heart like a hot branding iron. As it did Anna's. How shocked Mrs. Percy would be to discover the secret, impossible longing of Anna's heart.

"I expect he'll be visiting here soon."

Anna ducked her head rather than face the woman and try and guess what she meant by that statement. Everyone knew she and Colby had been friends at one time. Before he had left her to cope with her sorrow on her own.

Just as everyone knew he was Dorrie's father.

Caution kept her from mentioning Colby's visit.

The quilt was finished. The ladies rolled it and left it for Anna to complete. As they settled in to visit, Anna slipped to the kitchen to prepare the tea.

Her friend Laura followed her. "Baby needs nursing." She sat in a nearby chair and fed her newborn daughter.

"You look tired."

"It will take time for the baby to sleep through the night. In the meantime—" She shrugged.

"How is Adam feeling about Gloria?" She wondered if the three-year-old felt pushed out by the demands of his new sister.

"Carl takes Adam with him as much as he can. Adam loves it." Laura gave Anna a long considering look. "Has he been here?"

Anna knew she meant Colby but she pretended otherwise. "Adam or Carl?"

Laura only laughed. "You know who I mean."

"He was here."

"Drunk?"

He hadn't staggered or slurred his words. Officially she'd have to say he wasn't drunk. For all that was worth. "Says he's changed." She sounded every bit as weary as she felt.

"Has he?"

"How would I know? Saying so doesn't make it so, does it?"

"What did he want?"

Anna's gaze slid toward the little girl playing on the floor. "To see her."

"Only *see* her?" The concern in Laura's voice matched Anna's worry.

"That's all he said but…"

"What are you going to do?"

Anna relaxed and grinned. "Why, I thought I'd hand her over without a word."

Laura laughed. "And if I believe that you could sell me roosters as laying hens. Is he likely to let it go without a fight? How long do you suppose it will take for him to give up and go away? You know him as well as anyone. What's your guess?"

How well did she know him?

They'd enjoyed so many good times—wandering down by the river sharing secrets and fears. She'd counted on him for support and understanding but when her whole world had fallen apart and she needed him he'd disappeared. She'd waited for him to come. Her heart ached more with each passing day.

The final bit of bottom had fallen out of her world when she discovered he'd left town. She'd had to deal with the accident on her own.

The memory of it lived forever in her mind, in vivid color and sharp sounds. A wagon skidding on one wheel for what seemed a very long time. The scream of horses. The terrified cries of a woman with a baby clutched to her chest. She'd watched, powerless to stop the accident. Then in scenes so slow, so detailed she knew she would never erase them from her mind, the wagon hit a rock, flipped skyward, tipped over and landed upside-down. The woman flew through the air, landing with a heart-stopping thud. Then only the wheels moved, turning round and round.

She thought they would never quit.

She'd remained frozen to the spot until warm, demanding arms drew her away.

Her beloved stepmother, Rose, had died. As had baby Timmy.

She sucked in air and pushed away the memory, barring it from her thoughts.

At sixteen she had become a mother to Alex, six years her junior, and she had taken over her father's household.

And Colby had left. He didn't come for the funeral. He didn't come to offer comfort. He didn't come to share her fears. He returned eighteen months later with a wife soon to have a baby. Nora had died giving birth to Dorrie and Colby had thrust the newborn into Anna's arms.

She shouldn't have been surprised when Colby left a second time even though she could blame herself. She told him to leave. What she'd meant was for him to change his ways.

She no longer held out hope of him doing so and with decisiveness, shut her heart against caring, against hurting, and answered Laura's question. "He's never been one to stick around when things get difficult."

"Then I expect he'll soon be gone again."

The thought should have been comforting. Instead it sliced through her heart like an out-of-control butcher knife. She turned away lest Laura guess at her turmoil. Why did she still care even after all the pain he'd brought to her life?

Thankfully there wasn't time to discuss the matter further. Nor mull over silent questions. The ladies waited.

As she served tea and cakes, fourteen-year-old Alex came in from school. She went to the kitchen to speak to him.

"Come and say hello."

"Do I have to?" He shuddered, headed for the back door and escape, his face alternating between a flush and pallor.

She knew how he struggled with social occasions but he must learn to do what was proper. "Yes, you do. It's common courtesy." She wished she could inject Alex with some self-confidence but every effort she made only seemed to cause him to pull back more quickly. She rested a hand lightly on his shoulder and steered him to the parlor where the ladies enjoyed tea and visiting. "Just say hello and then you can play with Dorrie."

"'Lo." It was barely audible and more of a mumble than anything.

She ached for the way he shied away from people, preferring to live with his books and toys. She'd done her best for him but she knew nothing about raising a child.

Rose had married Father when Anna was almost five. Rose had brought joy and love into both Father's and Anna's life. After her death, Father had withdrawn into his Bible study.

Not, Anna realized, unlike Alex and his withdrawal from people.

Alex played with Dorrie a few minutes before he sidled up to Anna. "Can I go now?" he whispered.

She nodded.

As he slipped away, Dorrie protested loudly because her favorite playmate had left.

Anna picked up Dorrie to quiet her and realized every eye watched her. They had been talking about her. And decided she needed their helpful, friendly advice. She shifted her gaze to Mrs. Percy, expecting she would be the self-appointed spokeswoman. When Laura reached out and squeezed Anna's hand, Anna understood she wasn't going to like what she was about to hear.

Mrs. Percy adjusted her posture so she looked

even more imperious than ever, which had always been enough to strike fear into Anna's heart. "What's to be done about the cross?"

Anna knew she meant the wooden cross that graced the wall behind the pulpit. It had been badly damaged by the fire. She wondered what the women thought should be done about it.

"We obviously need a new one." Mrs. Percy spoke as if it had been firmly decided.

She thought of the burned cross and how important it had been in her life. "When you think of how the cross saves us from the flames…" She meant in a spiritual sense but seeing the confusion on the faces of the women around her, she knew they didn't understand, perhaps thought she meant the cross had somehow stopped the fire from consuming the church.

She didn't finish her thought but if there were any way possible, she'd salvage the cross. Not because Mr. Steves had been the one to hang it on the wall. Not because it was part of the original decoration, but because of what it meant to her.

But it was not the cross, nor repairs to the church that crowded her mind after the ladies left. It was Mrs. Percy's report of Colby's behavior.

He hadn't changed.

Colby would never be the man she needed and ached for.

She must persuade Father to talk to Colby, make him see the harm his presence was doing and convince him to leave town.

She would talk to Father tonight as soon as Alex and Dorrie were in bed.

Chapter Three

But it was the next morning before she got an opportunity to speak to her father. He surprised her with an announcement.

"Father, you didn't?" She had no right to question Father, but it took all her rigid self-control to keep from revealing the depth of her shock.

"I think it is an excellent idea. It takes care of many problems at the same time." He nodded as if completely satisfied with his decision and settled before the desk in the front room where he opened his Bible and prepared to turn his thoughts to study.

Anna stared at the contents of the room—the wooden armchair now back to its normal place beside the desk, the small table with a lamp and stack of pleasure books, the brown leather sofa that seemed best suited for decoration rather than comfort, the bookshelves holding Father's precious library, the ornately framed daguerreotypes—one of Rose and Father's wedding and the other of her own mother whom she barely remembered. She saw nothing in the contents of the room to calm her fears.

"How does hiring Colby solve any problems?"

"Isn't it obvious, dear daughter? He will get the repairs done to the church on time, leaving me to attend to other things. He'll be close enough to get to know Dorrie."

Exactly. Close enough to make it impossible to keep him from seeing her. And who knows what he'd want next? How that solved anything, Anna could not begin to understand.

"The young man and I had a good talk. I believe he's sincere in wanting to change. Who better to help him than us? Isn't that what the church is for? To provide help for those who need it?" He sent Anna a gently reproving look that brought a flood of guilt to war with her anger and fear.

"Of course but…"

Father smiled gently. "Don't give up on him. Nor disregard the Lord's work in his life."

Tears burned the back of Anna's eyes. It wasn't that she didn't have faith in God and what He could do, but believing in Colby had brought her nothing but pain and disappointment. She could not survive another shattering experience with him—trusting him, loving him against her best intentions, only to watch him ride away. Or worse, hear after days of waiting and wondering that he'd left town.

"By the way, he'll be sharing our meals."

Anna gasped.

Father's eyes flashed a challenge. "Are we not to show hospitality?"

"Yes, Father." She knew when to accept the inevitable but how would she cope? "When does he begin?"

"He's over there as we speak. He'll join us for lunch."

Colby hoped Anna would slip over to the church and speak to him. But it was her father who wandered over at lunchtime to invite him to join them. Colby followed across the yard with a mixture of anticipation and dread. No doubt being tossed out of the saloon had been duly reported to her. No one would believe that Colby Bloxham had been defending a helpless old man. They'd think he was drunk and rowdy as he once would have been.

But a stronger, more insistent emotion prevailed. He wanted to sit at the same table as Anna, have a chance to watch her, enjoy the sound of her voice.

He took the place Anna indicated—to the left of

Pastor Caldwell and across from Alex, who rushed in from school to join them. Anna sat opposite her father.

He didn't miss the fact his plate had been shoved as far away from Anna as possible but it only served to allow him opportunity to study her without the risk of being caught staring. She wore her hair in a roll at the back of her head. Supposed it was more in keeping with her role as the pastor's homemaker than letting it fall down her back as he remembered—the sun catching in it like gold glinting in a river. He'd already had a chance to see her eyes. Not that he needed any reminder. Light brown. There was a time they would look at him with warmth like a banked fire instead of coal-like coldness he now received.

Anna turned the high chair where Dorrie sat so the baby had her back to him. At Dorrie's protest he understood his daughter didn't like it any more than he did. He wanted to be able to study this little scrap of humanity he'd had a part in creating.

He met Anna's considering look. Saw the challenge in her eyes. Seems every time he tried to be different, something jerked him back to his old ways. But this time he'd run as far as he dared. He'd seen where he could end up.

He pulled his thoughts away from the journey that readied him to return. And away from the despicable deeds he had done. If Anna heard them…well, he could only hope she wouldn't.

Anna had often begged him to stop drinking and take a role in raising his daughter. His response had been to hit the trail with a bottle in his hand.

But that was over and he was back.

He felt Alex eyeing him under the shield of his lashes. The boy had grown considerably since Colby last saw him, though he was still small and puny. And lacking in confidence if the way he kept his head down indicated anything. Colby had learned to never duck his head, always fix a man with a bold, defiant stare, but then he supposed Alex didn't have any of the reasons Colby had for the way he viewed the world.

The strain in Alex's posture and Anna's averted eyes scraped along Colby's nerves, magnified by the way Dorrie fussed because she had to face the stove.

"She ain't invisible," he muttered. "I see her fine. She's got real purty hair."

Dorrie squirmed, trying to turn around. Then she kicked her heels against the chair legs. It sounded like she said, "Mama, wanna see." She threw her head back and shrieked.

No mistaking the determination in her voice, tinged with a pout. *That child needs a cuff alongside her ear.*

The words bellowed through his head in a voice he recalled from his past—his pa's. How often had he heard it and felt the blow that followed.

His insides tightened in a familiar response, ready to duck or run and if that failed, to fight back. He forced himself to relax and something unfamiliar in its insistency edged past the words from his past. He wouldn't run if someone tried to hit that little girl.

He'd left his baby daughter with Anna and her father, knowing they were good, gentle Christian people who, he hoped, would not treat the baby harshly. Yet he knew many good people believed in a strong hand with children. Conquer their spirit. Spare the rod and spoil the child. He understood the need for discipline but he hoped Anna had found a way to do it gently and kindly.

He had no idea how he would handle the situation other than to cuff the child. His nerves remained tense as he watched to see what she would do.

Anna took Dorrie's hands and spoke gently. "Dorrie, sweetie, you must not speak to Mama like that." She held the baby's hands until Dorrie settled down.

The air in Colby's lungs released in a hot blast. Her kind correction of Dorrie caught him somewhere between his rib cage and his gut. He'd forgotten how gentle her stepmother had been, even when she felt it necessary to speak to Colby regarding his behavior. In fact, he only now realized she'd been correcting him. Her words were so soft he'd welcomed them. Only other correction he'd had had come by way of Pa's fists. His insides twisted with remembrance of his pa's anger. He would not be like his old man. He would never hit that little girl. No matter how angry he got.

The hitting ended with him.

He bent over his plate, forcing himself to concentrate on his food as he pushed aside the bad memories.

Anna was a good cook. A man learned to appreciate fluffy homemade bread, rich brown gravy and a variety of vegetables.

"You do all those bad things they say?"

Colby jerked his head up at Alex's question. Had news of his activities reached Steveville? Or was it only gossip and speculation? If they heard the whole truth…

"Alex." Anna kept her voice soft but couldn't disguise her shock.

"It's fine."

Anna's quick glance said plainly it wasn't so far as she was concerned, but Colby figured he might as well deal with the spoken and unspoken questions right up-front.

"I don't know what all folks are saying about me but I did things I shouldn't have. Things I wish now I hadn't done. But that's behind me."

"God is good. He waits for his sons and daughters to return to Him," Pastor Caldwell said.

Colby nodded. He and the preacher had had a good talk. Colby had soaked in the words of love and forgiveness the preacher read from God's word and Colby had chosen to accept God's forgiveness for his sin, but Colby wasn't sure he'd go so far as to call himself a child of God. After all, God must have pretty high standards about who could be part of His family.

Dorrie mumbled something softly. He guessed she pleaded to be turned around. He wanted to add his pleas to hers but clearly Anna didn't care that he ached to see his daughter. Anna's lack of welcome hurt more than a fist to his face. Not that he would let it deter him. He was back. He had changed. He intended to prove it.

"Very well, seeing as you've been so good." She turned the high chair around.

Anna had always responded positively to gentle prodding. Colby remembered that about her. As clearly as he remembered so many other things.

He stared at Dorrie. She had his dark blond hair and his blue eyes. She had Nora's mouth and nose. And his directness. She stared unblinkingly at him and his heart sank to the pit of his stomach where it turned over twice and spun around leaving him struggling to fill his lungs. This was his child. Flesh of his flesh.

"You gonna take her away?" Alex demanded.

Colby noted Anna didn't correct his curiosity this time.

The pastor leaned forward. "Colby has explained his intentions to me but perhaps—" he faced Colby "—for Alex and Anna's peace of mind, you could tell them, as well."

Colby nodded. "I had to make sure she was okay. And I intend to start over right here."

Anna fixed a look on him. Her expression was composed but, though he guessed she tried, she failed to hide her anger. "Haven't you done this before?"

"Anna," her father warned. "He is a guest in our house. I believe he deserves a chance. After all, what would God want us to do?"

Anna ducked her head but not before Colby could understand she didn't think he deserved another chance.

He had his job cut out proving to her he meant it for real. But now was not the time or place to discuss it. Perhaps if he hung about he might later get a chance to explain things to her.

He turned his attention back to Dorrie. "It's

amazing to see bits of myself and Nora in her." Conviction burrowed into his thoughts. He wanted to be part of this child's life. He wanted to watch her grow and change. He wanted to teach her to channel that boldness he saw in her gaze, use it for good and not ill.

Anna put her arm around Dorrie's shoulders as if she could shield the child from his stare.

He ducked his head and tried to concentrate on his food. His throat felt thick as he understood her fear that he would take Dorrie from her. He didn't want to do that. A man alone wasn't the way to raise a proper little girl. But he did want to be part of Dorrie's life and he didn't know how best to do that. Was being in Steveville, proving himself changed, enough? He couldn't say.

"How do you purpose to begin work at the church?" the pastor asked.

It took a great deal of effort for Colby to force his thoughts to the fire-damaged church. "The first thing I need to do is tear out and burn the damaged wall then begin to rebuild."

"Father, everyone is expecting the church to be reopened in time for the birthday celebration." Anna spoke softly, but Colby heard a cautious note in her voice.

Pastor Caldwell explained about the birthday party for the town's founding father.

"When is it to be?"

"June seventeen."

"A month away." Colby considered it a moment, mentally measuring the work to be done. "Shouln't be a problem to finish by then." From his quick study of the damage he figured he could finish in ten days or a little more if he really pushed it. He shot a quick glance at Dorrie, shifted his gaze to Anna. Seemed no reason to hurry.

"You'll burn everything damaged by the fire?" Anna sounded cautious.

He wondered what she wanted but didn't care to ask directly. "Seems the best thing to do. Why?"

"Just curious."

Distracted by the way Dorrie continued to stare at him, he let it go. Besides, he figured if Anna didn't want to tell him what she wanted, he wouldn't prod it from her. He knew beneath her gentle, patient exterior lay a streak of stubbornness to challenge most mules.

Dorrie lifted one hand toward him. "Da-da."

Her word slammed through his insides, reverberating against his ribs, resounding inside his head.

Anna gave a short laugh as she grabbed Dorrie's hands and pushed them to the tray. "She calls every man that. It's a little embarrassing. Except Father, she calls him poppa. I don't know how many times

she's called a perfect stranger da-da. If people
didn't know better they might think…" She trailed
off as if realizing she'd been running over at the
mouth.

Dorrie flashed him a smile and turned to the
pastor. "My poppa."

Pastor Caldwell chuckled. "My Dorrie. You're
a little minx, aren't you?"

Dorrie babbled something.

Colby wondered if anyone else understood what
she said. He didn't but he grinned simply because
her pleasure was contagious. He shifted his gaze to
Anna, wanting to share the moment, but her eyes
challenged him so directly his enjoyment deflated.

Anna rightly wondered how his presence
affected her role as Dorrie's mama. She had every
reason in the world to wonder if he'd run again at
the first sign of trouble.

He was determined he would not. But he would
have to prove it.

Chapter Four

Not until the door closed after Colby did Anna's nerves stop twitching. She watched out the window as he strode down the road to the right. Where was he going? Apparently it was too much to hope he'd leave town now rather than later after they all started thinking he might stay.

But at least he was out of her house, out of her sight. Just not out of her thoughts. Try as she had over the months, she could never get him completely out of her thoughts.

"Anna, what if he does want to take Dorrie?" Alex's voice thinned with worry—a worry that scratched the inside of her mind, as well.

Father appeared in the doorway. "He says he doesn't. Do we have any reason to doubt his word?" Carrying his Bible Father left to visit a family whose mother lay sick.

Anna could think of many reasons for mistrusting what Colby said—and even more for not counting on him. Experience had taught her those cruel lessons. But it had not taught her a way to subdue the portion of her heart that longed for the closeness they had shared. It had been a childhood friendship. Nothing more. But she couldn't stop the yearning in her heart that wanted to reignite that friendship. Feel again the closeness, the bond, the instant understanding they once had.

Only her rigid, well-honed self-control enabled her to dismiss such foolishness and turn her attention back to Alex's need. She squeezed his shoulder. "Alex, we can pray and trust God to be in control of the situation."

Alex skittered a sideways look at her. "I'm afraid." He ducked his head so he spoke into his chest. "Sometimes bad things happen."

She pulled him to her side, wanting to assure him he was safe. But how could she? He'd lost more than she when his mother and baby brother had died. "We have to trust God knows best." She had fought a hard battle in her heart to get to the place where she could trust God again. Alex lacked her adult perspective to rationalize events and apply faith. His thin shoulder pressed into her ribs but he remained stiff as a stick.

Knowing she had nothing more to offer than words, she released him and turned to wash Dorrie's face.

Her disobedient thoughts returned to Colby and the way he'd edged his way into Father's good graces. Father believed in extending forgiveness, which was fine in theory. Not so great when it put so many people at risk. Father would be shocked at the words biting the back of Anna's tongue. If she voiced her thoughts he would gently chide her for being uncharitable, for not showing the love of God.

Alex's mouth remained in a tight line. His eyes clouded with troublesome thoughts.

Her heart went out to her younger brother. "Alex, I'm sure there's no reason to worry." She wished it were so. "Now help me with the dishes and then you can start your homework." She lifted Dorrie from her chair. As soon as Dorrie's feet hit the floor she went to Alex and babbled something, her face wreathed in concern as if sensing his uncertainty.

He scooped her into his arms and tickled her, making her giggle.

"Lexie," she protested, but they all knew she loved it as much as Alex.

Anna watched the pair. Not only did she have her heart to protect, she must shield these two children from hurt, as well. She constructed a quick, impenetrable shell around the thoughts that remembered happier times with Colby. She could not let them divert her from her present concerns.

Later, as she helped Alex with his homework, she resolutely kept that shell in place. One effective way to do so was to think of the cross hanging on the fire-scarred wall. So many things raced through her mind—the times she'd knelt before that cross, giving her problems and struggles to the Lord, seeking His help in dealing with the loss of Rose, the challenges of raising her younger brother and running her father's home. How frightened she'd been when Colby had thrust his newborn baby into Anna's arms and begged her to take care of it.

At first, her prayer had been for Colby to stay, stop his foolish behavior and become a true partner in the raising of his daughter. Her cheeks burned as she recalled how she'd imagined him confessing his love and asking her to marry him. She now understood he could not be the man she needed. She'd done her best to accept it and focus her thoughts on being a mother to the two children in her care and running her father's household efficiently. *God, why did You let him come back when I was sure I had put thoughts of him behind me?*

She wanted to slip over to the church as she'd done so often and find help, strength and renewal of her faith at the foot of the cross. It meant more to her than a symbol of Christ's death. It was a visible reminder of God's faithfulness in her life.

Despite Mrs. Percy's edict, Anna couldn't bear the thought of having the cross burned along with the rest of the debris, especially now when she knew her faith and resolve were about to be tested yet again by Colby's return.

She'd always found what she needed in prayer and she turned her thoughts toward God in a burst of faith. *God, my first concern is protecting Dorrie. And I need Your wisdom to do that. But I also need to rest in Your strength as I face Colby each day. Help me be faithful to what You've called me to do.*

Calm returned to her soul for the first time in many hours. God had always been faithful and loving as she struggled with her many doubts and fears. It was as if He patiently held out His arms, welcoming her after each bout of uncertainty.

She wanted to save that cross. It was only a piece of wood but was a monument to her—a sweet reminder of all the times she'd turned to God for help and received more than she asked or dreamed.

Once Dorrie was sleeping she could leave. "Alex, listen for Dorrie while I run over to the church."

Each Sunday she accompanied Father on the piano as he led the song service so she often ran over to practice on the church piano. Only this time her interest wasn't in music.

As she stepped into the dim interior she breathed in the acrid smell of the fire still clinging to the air, but it failed to rob her of the peace and tranquility she felt in this place. She moved slowly up the center aisle pausing to wipe her fingers along the top of one of the wooden pews. She checked her fingertips, saw a trace of dust. She'd tried to keep the place clean after the fire even though it wasn't used for services. Somehow it seemed sacrilegious to let dust accumulate. Besides not only did she pray and play the piano here, Father still came over to study and pray.

She arrived at the front. The pulpit had been taken to the meeting place so nothing obstructed her view of the cross or the blackened wall. Raw wood had been nailed over the bottom where the fire had broken through. She climbed the three steps to the platform, her heels thudding on the wood, and stood in front of the cross. The foot had been burned off completely and much of what remained was blackened by smoke or charred by the fire.

Her vision blurred. She couldn't explain it in words but she felt the cross surviving the flames was a visible lesson of a spiritual truth—that Jesus's death had spared them all from the flames of judgment.

She scrubbed at her eyes. This was a lesson she wanted to share even as much as she wanted to preserve the cross that had such significance in her life.

She slid her fingers along the wood, carefully going with the grain to avoid slivers. It fit tightly to the wall. She wouldn't be able to simply lift it off.

If she could only see how it was secured but the evening light had faded to a gentle dove-gray.

"Figuring to steal it?"

She jerked back and caught her finger against a rough patch as she spun around to see who spoke. A sliver dug into her flesh. "Ouch." She squeezed her finger to stop the pain.

Colby stood before her, a grin splitting his face.

She scowled. "It's you. I should have guessed." It would be too much by far to think he'd wandered down the street and found some place miles away to hang out. She gritted her teeth but not before the barest moan escaped.

He shifted his amused gaze to her hands and sobered. "Are you hurt?" He grabbed her finger and bent over to examine it.

Heat scalded her throat and cheeks at his touch. A thousand dreams and wishes blossomed like flowers after a rain. She knew she should protest and pull away but she stood as immobile as a slab of clay.

He turned her finger gently toward the last bit of light from the west-facing windows. He probed the site with a light touch then yanked out the sliver.

She gasped yet welcomed the sudden pain. The flowers withered and died and saneness returned. There were no dreams, no wishes with this man.

He pressed the site, ending the pain as quickly as it came. Then he squeezed the tip of her finger. "A little blood flow will wash away the dirt." Two drops of blood plopped to the oiled wood of the floor. She'd have to scrub it off later.

He watched her finger a heartbeat longer. "I think I got it all but you best wash it thoroughly when you get home." When he released her hand she couldn't seem to move. She stared at her arm suspended between them, felt the heat from her cheeks spread to her hairline and scald the roots of her hair. She yanked her arm to her waist. Her heart throbbed where the sliver had been.

He leaned back, his head bare.

At least he had the decency to remove his hat in God's house. She realized her thoughts were uncharitable but found perverse strength in them.

"So what were you doing?" he asked.

"Looking."

"Don't get slivers by looking."

"So I touched it." She had no intention of telling

this man anything more than that. "What are you doing here?"

He chuckled. "I was enjoying a quiet evening." He sounded vaguely regretful, as if her presence had spoiled his solitude.

"Maybe you could enjoy it somewhere else. Don't you have friends you can stay with or something?"

"You suggesting I go to the saloon?" His quiet words challenged her. "I seem to remember a time when you begged me to stay away from that sort of company."

"That was a long time ago. Things have changed."

"I'm glad you admit it. Because—" he leaned close "—I've changed. Didn't you promise to pray for me? Did you do it? Or decide I was a lost cause?" His nose was only inches from hers. "Perhaps you prayed I would never return."

She refused to step back and let him intimidate her. Instead she drew herself up tall and tipped her chin. "I did pray for you. At first."

He nodded. "Then you decided to give up on me?"

She narrowed her eyes. "Then I prayed you'd never come back and embarrass Dorrie with your sinful ways."

He straightened and stepped back.

Even in the fading light she glimpsed what she

could only take for as hurt. She almost regretted her honest words then he grinned and she didn't regret them one bit. The man was far too blasé about life. Just as he was about responsibilities and friend-ships.

Not even to herself would she admit it was one of the things she had enjoyed about him—his ability to smile through troubles, laugh at adversity and enjoy life.

"Sorry to disappoint you." He shifted to stare past her. "What would the good people of the church say if they knew you tried to steal the cross? Do you suppose your father would be embar-rassed?"

"This is ridiculous. It's a burned piece of wood. Aren't you planning to burn it tomorrow?"

"So what were you doing?"

He wasn't about to leave the topic alone. But neither was she prepared to share her emotional at-tachment to the cross. It would make sense to no one else. They would see only how it was burned, damaged beyond repair. Mrs. Percy was right. It should be destroyed. But a flurry of regrets swamped her at the thought.

"Something hidden behind it maybe? Some-thing you don't want anyone to discover?"

A dull churn of anger ignited at his accusation. She suspected he was purposely trying to annoy her. But how dare he suggest she might be guilty of doing anything wrong. She was a preacher's daughter who carefully lived a circumspect life. And if she ever missed the expectations of her role by so much as a hair there were plenty of people who would point it out to her. "I was only seeing if there was a way to salvage it." She lifted her skirts and descended the steps. "Obviously I am being foolishly sentimental. Might as well burn it and put up a new cross." As she hurried down the aisle, she struggled to control this unfamiliar indignation.

She marched across the yard and into the house. There wasn't time to dwell on her unexpected reaction to Colby. She planned to finish the quilt tonight and deliver it as soon as possible. Thankfully the evenings had been warm enough of late, but if they had a cold, damp spell the Andersons would be hard-pressed to keep warm with the few things they've been given.

Anna paused as she sewed the edging on. She thought of how close she had come to sharing Hazel Anderson's situation. The fire had been within inches… She shuddered. Life was so uncertain.

She jabbed the needle through the layers of the quilt with unusual vigor. Father might feel charitable toward Colby Bloxham. But all she felt was an enormous need to get the man on his way as soon as humanly possible before he upset her life. Again.

She needed divine help and paused to bow her head. *Our Father in heaven, be so kind as to put Your mighty hand on the man's back and move him onward. Before he turns my world upside down and my heart inside out. Again.*

Chapter Five

Anna woke the next morning with a heavy feeling in her limbs. She wanted to believe it was because the night had been unbearably hot. Or because the wind wailed and moaned around the house like a woman in mourning yet did nothing to relieve the heat.

But it was not the warm air or tormented wind that prevented Anna from sleeping.

She had mentally scolded herself far into the night.

Why did she still react to Colby with the same swift pleasure and longing as she had when she was young and foolish?

Why had she let Colby affect her so she said such a foolish thing as burn the cross? Not that the cross mattered except to her.

But his intentions regarding Dorrie did matter. Would he take the child? Could he? She gave a snort of disbelief. Who in their right mind would let him? And she didn't mean just herself. The town would rise up and stop him. Colby Bloxham raising a little girl?

With sluggish inefficiency she prepared breakfast and tended to Dorrie. It was Saturday so she left Alex sleeping. She didn't feel up to coping with his reluctance to do his assigned chores even though she suspected he would open his eyes, turn to his back and read as soon as she stepped from his room. She shrugged. What did it matter if he enjoyed a few relaxing moments?

She turned her thoughts back to the cross. During the night she had made up her mind. The cross might mean nothing special to anyone else but it did to her and she wanted to keep it. As soon as breakfast was over she'd take a hammer and screwdriver and figure out a way to get it off the wall before Colby could follow her rash instructions.

Father returned from his morning prayers, his step light. He'd plainly enjoyed his time with God.

She needed some time alone with her Lord, as well. Time to pull her worries into submission. Time to find her peace.

Knowing Colby might show up any moment to

start repairs, the church would no longer be a place of refuge for her.

Another reason to resent the man's reappearance in her life.

She sighed inwardly, her weariness increasing with each moment.

Breakfast was almost ready and she called Alex but didn't wait for him to get dressed before she informed Father the meal was ready and put Dorrie in her chair. Neither of them could bear to wait for their morning meal.

As she helped Dorrie with her glass of milk she suddenly paused and lifted her head. "Do you smell something burning?" Since the fire any hint of smoke sent her scurrying to check the nearby buildings, her heart twisting with fear. The flames had come dangerously close to the house. She'd never been so afraid nor prayed so hard. God had answered that prayer.

God had turned the tragedy into blessing in many ways—people had come back to Him like prodigal sons, cause for much rejoicing in many homes.

She raced to the window without waiting for an answer from Father about the smell of smoke. Flames licked skyward from the churchyard. "Fire," she called.

"It's probably Colby burning garbage." Father sounded so calm she knew he expected it.

"He's at the church already?"

"He was there when I arrived. Already had some boards pulled off the wall. Seems eager to get the work done."

As she stared out the window, Colby sauntered over and tossed some boards into the flames. He'd filled out over the years. Looked like he could handle any physical challenge. She blinked back a hard stinging in her eyes. He could certainly toss an armload of wood but could he handle problems? How long before something sent him riding out of town? Again.

Then she realized what he was doing.

The cross. She thought she'd have lots of time to rescue it. "Father, watch Dorrie. I have something to look after." She didn't wait for him to ask what was so important to take her away in the middle of serving a meal.

She picked up her skirts and ran to the back entrance of the church. She didn't slow until she faced the wall. The raw boards had been peeled away. Much of the damaged area had been knocked down. The cross was gone. She stood in ashes, disappointment burning through her veins.

Colby sauntered in, whistling through his teeth. "Morning." He picked up bits of wood.

"Where is it? Did you burn it?"

"Burn what?" He paused on his way to the door.

"The cross."

He grinned. "Thought you said to."

"I didn't mean it. I wanted to save it." She pressed her lips tight to stop a wail from escaping.

"Hang on a minute while I dump this armload." He disappeared out the door. She heard a clatter and caught a whiff of smoke.

She hadn't moved. Didn't know if she could. Her failure left her stunned and immobile. It was only a piece of wood. She knew it had nothing to do with God's power, His ability to answer prayer, His love or anything of importance. She didn't need the cross to communicate with Him. Or hear Him speak through His holy word. She knew all that. The cross had no significance except as a sentimental reminder of all He'd done.

She heard Colby return but didn't bother looking at him. The shard of annoyance she felt toward him was foolish and out of place. He'd only done what she said. She'd been rash in her words and regretted it from the moment she'd uttered them.

"Come with me. I have something to show you."

She shook her head. She wasn't interested in anything he had.

He grasped her elbow, gently turning her about.

His touch fired up her nerves like flames. She jerked back. She didn't want him touching her.

Didn't want him reawakening feelings and awareness she'd fought so fiercely to quell.

But he wasn't about to let her discourage him. He again took her elbow, a little more firmly, and steered her relentlessly toward the back into the cloakroom. Only so he would leave her alone did she let him drag her along. "Look," he said.

Her eyes widened like Dorrie's would if given a gift. Her heart resurrected from the pit of her stomach and exploded against her ribs. "The cross." The words blasted from her. Fractured, it leaned in an empty corner.

She rushed over and touched it to assure herself she wasn't imagining it. "I thought you burned it."

He shrugged. "You said to. But I figured there was something special about it. Didn't find any money behind it. Not even a long lost letter from some beau—" He chuckled at the pained look she sent his way. "So I figured it was the cross itself you wanted."

She nodded, unable to find words beyond her surprise.

"What do you want me to do with it?"

She knelt to examine it more closely. The fire damage was worse than she thought. "I wanted to save it." She sat back on her heels and swallowed a lump of disappointment. "I guess I thought there must be some way to repair it, restore it. I didn't realize how badly it's damaged." She pushed to her feet. "Leave it here. Maybe I'll figure out something." She couldn't bear the thought of burning it even though it seemed the only thing to do.

Turning, she came face-to-face with him, staring into his blue eyes. Found it impossible to sort out her feelings. He'd understood this piece of burned wood meant something to her and saved it. His insight surprised her, shifted her thoughts so she wasn't able to maintain her anger toward him. "Thank you," she murmured. "It was kind of you to save it."

His eyes blazed with amusement. "I'm really a nice guy."

She couldn't break away from his gaze, knew a jab of regret that what they once shared no longer existed. There was a time she would have told him her doubts and fears. He would have told her his dreams. Just as he'd told her about the harshness he'd suffered at the hands of his father.

She blinked. Seems he could never run far enough to escape that memory. She tried to protect herself with such knowledge yet something soft as warm butter had eased her anger. "You didn't come for breakfast," she murmured.

"I didn't know if I was welcome."

Guilty as accused. For the moment she couldn't remember why she should have made him feel so cautious. "It's not too late."

He nodded, a tangle of hope and caution filling his expression. "I'll be over then."

She stepped away, sucked in smoke-laden air that seemed lacking in oxygen, and hurried to the yard, the smoke out there even heavier. No wonder she couldn't breathe normally. In the house, she placed another plate on the table. She heard Father moving about and went to inform him Colby would be over and suggested he keep him company.

Father sorted through some books, no doubt looking for a commentary or something.

She glanced around the room. "Where's Dorrie?"

He looked up, surprise widening his eyes. "She was just here."

Anna resisted an urge to roll her eyes. Father could become so focused on something the world could fall down around his feet and he'd barely notice.

"Dorrie," she called.

"She's with me." Alex's voice came from his bedroom.

The impact of what she'd just done hit her so hard she groaned.

"Something wrong?" Father asked.

"No." Not in the sense he meant. But she'd extended a welcome to a man who not only could tear out her heart but rip her family apart, as well.

She scrambled to think how she could undo her foolish deed.

She hurried to Alex's bedroom. Dorrie's head lay close to his on the pillow and she scrunched up beside him peering at the book he read to her.

"Keep Dorrie here for a bit, would you?"

Alex lowered the book to look at Anna. "How come?"

"Colby is coming for breakfast and—" She sent a warning look in Dorrie's direction.

"Sure. We're going to finish reading this book, aren't we, Dorrie?"

Dorrie babbled something, pointing at one of the pictures and Anna hurried out, grateful for Alex's understanding.

Knowing Dorrie would be safe from Colby for a bit longer, her heart grew lighter and she sang the words to one of Issac Watt's hymns, "Alas! and did my Savior bleed?" as she fried more potatoes and eggs and sliced more bread.

She could protect Dorrie. *Thank you, God.*

The cross had been saved. *Thank God.*

And thank Colby? a fragile voice whispered.

She'd thanked him. Even invited him to breakfast against her better judgment. And she'd thank him good and proper…

When he waved goodbye as he rode from town, leaving them in peace.

Colby tapped on the door then stepped inside and quietly sat at the table. Father poured them coffee. Colby glanced past her as if searching for Dorrie.

She sent him a look intended to inform him he could eat at her table, rescue the cross she attached sentimental value to, maybe even renew bits and pieces of their old friendship, but he needn't expect her to let him see Dorrie if she could help it.

She wouldn't stand by and let him gaze at the child with the longing and sadness she'd seen last night.

"Mama." Dorrie raced into the room, Alex hot on her heels.

"She wouldn't stay." He sent Colby a curious look before he ducked his head, hiding his face.

Anna scooped up Dorrie hoping to whisk her away before she saw Colby. But she was too late.

"Da-da," Dorrie gurgled, adding a whole lot more that no one understood.

Anger—as unfamiliar as palm trees, as powerful as the fire that destroyed the buildings down the street—raged through Anna. Anger directed as much at herself as at Colby. She'd put Dorrie at risk. But he had no right to come back. Not even if God had changed him, something she wasn't yet ready to believe.

Oh, Lord, forgive me. I rejoice that one of Your

lambs that was lost has been found. But why, God, did he have to come back here? Couldn't he just as well start over in California or Alaska?

She handed Dorrie to Alex and he carried her back to his room. Rather than sit at the table with Colby and Father, she remained at the cupboard, staring out the window at the flames consuming the old lumber from the church, a cloud of gray smoke billowing upward, blotting out all but a blue edge of the sky. Colby's presence had done the same for her, blotting out all but fragments of her normal peace of mind.

It was Saturday, one of her busiest days. The Sunday clothes had to be brushed and ironed; the shoes polished; and as Father insisted on observing a complete day of rest, every bit of food for Sunday prepared ahead of time. Normally she anticipated the coming day of rest with nothing much to do unless she counted caring for Dorrie and reading, neither of which constituted work in Anna's mind. But today she scurried about almost resenting the extra work Sunday required. She could find no peace in her heart or satisfaction in her chores. She ached for a chance to sit quietly before the cross and take her concerns to God, knowing she would find both comfort and guidance.

Instead, each time she glanced out the window,

she caught glimpses of Colby carrying more wood to the fire or standing back considering the building. She wished he would leave.

The idea cut through her. Not like he'd left before—far away and for many months. Just for the afternoon so she could enjoy a peaceful hour in the church.

Suddenly she realized she hadn't seen him for some time. She went to the open window and listened but heard no sound of work from inside the church. Nothing.

"Alex, watch Dorrie. Don't let her out of your sight. I'm going to run over to the church." She couldn't sit on a pew and meditate in front of the cross, but Father had given her the list of hymns a few days ago. She knew them all. Could play them with her eyes closed, but she'd go over them again. The music spoke to her soul as much as did prayer and Bible reading.

She tiptoed into the sanctuary and listened but didn't see or hear Colby. She sat at the piano and was soon lost in the music as she sang the familiar hymns with real joy. She finished and sat with her eyes closed, rejoicing in the beauty of the words, letting the peace they gave her fill her soul.

The sound of one person clapping jolted her eyes open. Colby sat in the nearest pew. "That was excellent."

"Thank you." She felt no gratitude, only annoyance as she left the piano bench and stood facing him. "Where have you been?" *How long have you been watching me?*

He grinned. "Did you miss me?"

"No and don't be facetious."

"I can't possibly be facetious seeing as I don't even know what it means."

"It means silly."

He tipped his head and smiled.

She wanted to believe it was a teasing, insincere smile but something serious lay behind the blue glitter of his eyes. Something that reached for her heart. Something her heart welcomed. She slammed shut an iron-clad mental door.

"I meant it. I enjoy your playing and singing."

He spoke in the present tense. Just like the days when he came to the church and listened as she practiced. Not until Rose died did she take over playing in the services. By then she knew the hymns by heart.

"I remember some of the church songs from when I used to come here."

Did he remember the way their hearts had seemed to beat a common song, finding so many things they both enjoyed, almost able to read each other's thoughts? Obviously it had meant more to her than him or he wouldn't have found it so easy to leave.

Why had he bothered to come back?

She fully believed he would leave again. He always left. The peace she had achieved drained out the bottom of her soul, leaving her edgy and unsettled.

"You sing them like they mean something real. I enjoyed it. You play even better than I remember."

People seldom commented on her playing unless she made a mistake. To hear words of praise melted a layer of her defensiveness.

"I envy you. Your life has always been filled with God's word, and songs such as these." Regret seemed to fill the crevices of his face.

His words gave her pause. Did he remember she'd told him God didn't care where they came from, only whether or not they were willing to allow His love into their lives? Basically, since his return, she'd been denying her belief in that truth and guilt burned through her. But it couldn't get past the hard shell she'd forged around her emotions. She'd trusted him too often and too easily and she wouldn't be doing it again.

"Yes, I've been blessed. I know that."

She wasn't about to dispute the beauty of the hymns, nor discuss the benefits of her upbringing, something else she could not dispute.

It took a concerted effort to pull her gaze away from his, which seemed so endless, so hungry, so—

she jerked her attention to the scarred wall at the back of the platform.

"I'll get out of your way so you can get to work." As she hurried to the house she wondered where he'd been when she first entered the church.

It wasn't until the door closed behind her that she wished she'd confronted him about Dorrie. What were his intentions? Was he about to snatch the child from her? At the idea, she moaned deep inside, beyond sound, beyond reason.

Chapter Six

Colby watched fine people in their fine clothes climb the outside wooden steps to the room above the saloon. He didn't own a suit or anything remotely like it. He wore the best of what he had— a new white shirt he'd purchased at the mercantile and his best pair of black trousers, brushed clean. But it didn't seem quite fitting. He felt more like his father's son than a changed man and fell back into the shadow of the mercantile store as he tried to decide if he would climb the steps or walk away and find something else to do with his time— something more fitting for a Bloxham.

Trouble was—he didn't know what a Bloxham determined to be different would do on a sunny Sunday morning apart from going to church like all decent people did.

Would the decent folk think he should be in their meeting place? Or would they think he fit better in the room below?

He brushed away a persistent fly and continued to watch people arrive.

A family hurried up the sidewalk, a man with a little boy in his arms and a young woman carrying a baby.

His heart bucked once before he tamed it. Family. Like he and Anna had both dreamed of. Would it ever be possible for him?

The man noticed him and headed over, his hand extended. "Carl Klaus." He waited for Colby to give his name and when he did, Carl nodded. "Welcome. Why don't you go up with us?"

His wife came to his side. "I'm Laura, Carl's wife. These are our children, Adam and Gloria. Perhaps you remember me. I'm Anna's friend. Have been since we were children."

Colby nodded a greeting, his hat gripped awkwardly in his fists. He remembered Laura hanging about when he was younger. Never paid her much attention. Guess he never really saw anyone but Anna and her family. They had been his whole world.

He wondered that Laura's friendship with Anna didn't make her a little less welcoming.

Wheezy organ music began.

"We better hurry," Karl said, and Colby allowed himself to be drawn along with the family, up the stairs and into the smoky interior of the room. He should have felt at home in such an atmosphere but his nerves twitched like a gun had been pressed to his spine. He was aware of glances aimed at him, full of doubt or even edged with condemnation. Not that he blamed any of them. He didn't belong here with these righteous folk. But he meant to start over as a man, and as a believer. And that meant attending church services.

His faith was new and untried, uncertain even, but he had prayed the sinner's prayer with Pastor Caldwell and he meant it. Soon enough they'd all see.

Colby Bloxham was done with running.

Colby Bloxham was different. Though he figured God might find him a bigger challenge than most.

Caught up in his thoughts, he'd blindly followed Carl and his family to the front row of seats before he realized where he was.

No way would he sit with nothing between him and the preacher. It left him too exposed. Not that he expected anyone could see what lay behind Colby but he wasn't taking any chances and quickly slid to the chair behind the Klaus family.

Alex already sat in the front row, holding

Dorrie's hand, and allowed her to edge close to Laura.

Dorrie turned, spotted Colby and flashed him a welcoming grin. His heart stomped over his doubts and headed straight for determination. He wanted to be part of this child's life. He'd do whatever necessary to gain that position.

He stole a glance about and saw many of the ladies pressed handkerchiefs to their noses. He tested the air, found it full of smoke and fumes from the saloon below—something he wouldn't have noticed if not for the obvious discomfort of the others.

More proof that Colby Bloxham did not fit here. But he settled down hard. He would learn to be comfortable. Might some day even feel he belonged.

Anna sat at the organ, pumping madly and playing songs he recognized from yesterday. He'd allowed himself only one glimpse at her as he entered the room. Now he ducked his head to study her from under cover of his lashes. So self-contained, so in control. Not at all like the girl he'd known prior to Rose's death. Would she remember how she'd told him she wondered if she would ever be what she should be and confessed a myriad of fears and what she thought were dreadful sins? How he'd laughed when she'd complained of her wicked temper. The worst thing she'd ever done was slam her bedroom door. She'd been shocked when he told her the things his old man did in anger.

She'd be equally shocked, if not more so, if she were ever to learn the things Colby had done.

He hoped she never would.

Pastor Caldwell announced the first hymn, bringing Colby gratefully from remembering things he wanted to forget.

He opened the hymnal and as they began to sing, he recognized the song—"Amazing Grace." Rose sang it often. Said she never got tired of the victory of the words.

Suddenly he missed Rose with an ache that sucked away all his resolve and indifference.

Rose had welcomed him into her home, treating him kindly. She'd touched his shoulder, ruffled his hair. He'd learned not to cringe when she touched him. Even found excuses to invite her gentle gestures. And then she'd died in a stupid senseless accident along with her tiny baby. He'd lost his own mother when she walked away from his old man's fists. He'd failed to stop her. But it hadn't hurt near as much as losing Rose.

Overflowing with sorrow, Colby sought Anna's face. Anna's loss had been even greater and he'd had nothing to offer her.

Afraid she'd discover the truth of how inadequate he was he'd left.

She met his eyes, their gazes locked as they sang together the words of the hymn. Was she remembering, too, hurting, too? He wanted to do something but again, just as when it happened, he failed to find anything to give.

The song ended and she jerked away to listen to her father, and then another number was given and she flipped the pages of the hymnal and focused on the notes.

Colby turned his attention to the words.

But even though he kept his head down, reading from the hymnal, he heard Anna's clear voice. Sweetness swept away bits of debris in his heart.

The song service ended and Anna left the organ bench to sit beside Laura, pulling Dorrie to her lap. Dorrie fussed a moment and kicked her little feet. Only because Colby watched so closely did he see Anna flinch.

He cringed, knowing if he'd done that, even as young as Dorrie, his pa would have smacked him hard. He remembered his ears ringing, his eyes smarting from the pain. He understood Dorrie must stop kicking but the thought of someone hitting her, even with a small hand like Anna's made him want to grab the child from her and run out the door.

Anna simply caught the thrashing feet and held them still until Dorrie settled.

Relief eased away his tension. His shoulders relaxed.

He stilled a jolt of surprise as he realized he had no idea how to be a father without being like his pa and he would sooner ride out into nowhere and camp there until he was old and gray than be that kind of father. He watched Dorrie settle into submission.

He wanted to be what he'd always wanted—a good father—but could he? Or would he fail as he had in the past?

Pastor Caldwell announced his text, "Deuteronomy, Chapter 10, Verse 12, 'What doth the Lord thy God require of thee, but to fear the Lord thy God, to walk in all His ways, and to love Him, and to serve the Lord thy God with all thy heart and with all thy soul.'" The pastor closed his thick Bible. In calm, thoughtful tones, Pastor Caldwell spoke about fearing God.

Colby certainly did that. Sort of thought God watched him to see if he would measure up. Colby figured to do his best to meet God's requirements.

As the pastor closed the meeting, Colby vowed he would do his best to please God and prayed it would be good enough.

And if it wasn't…

* * *

The next day he returned to work on the church, still mulling over the words of the sermon and what his response should be.

Last night he'd read the Bible until it grew too dark to see the words. He was going to change who Colby Bloxham was. According to what he read, God had given him a fresh start and God would help him be a better man.

He figured God had His hands full with that job.

But how to learn to be a father? He hadn't found an answer for that.

Nor had he found anything he could offer Anna. Maybe he never would. But he was here to stay. Perhaps in time he would discover something she needed that he could give.

He knew the minute she stepped from the house. Could tell by the way she hesitated and fumbled with the basin in her hands she had something specific in mind that involved him.

He knelt at the ragged foot of a stud he had cut out and waited. Pretending—every bit as good as she—that he wasn't so aware of her presence he couldn't remember if he'd driven in a spike or not.

She stepped closer, pausing. Out of the corner of his eyes he observed how she glanced back at the house and then seemed to push invisible iron rods down her backbone. He recognized that look and knew she intended to do business with him—business he suspected they both might find awkward.

She drew close, saw what he was doing and gasped. "What have you done? You were supposed to repair the hole. Instead you've made it larger."

He sat back on his heels. "The fire did more damage than you might think. I've had to take most of it down. The basic structure needs repair. Even some ceiling rafters."

"No one else thought that. You'll never finish if you keep tearing apart the place."

Her obvious shock at discovering he might be around longer than she'd originally believed left him cold and lonely. Such a contrast to the pleasant thoughts he'd been enjoying—remembering her singing so sweetly at church, remembering details of walks they'd taken and conversations they'd shared when they were but youngsters.

"You couldn't see it until you knocked off the plaster. I showed it to your father and he agreed it needed to be done." He watched her with unblinking patience, waiting for her response, hoping she might regret her initial reaction and voice some word of approval, if not for him then at least for the work he did.

"I thought—I wanted you—"

"You want me gone." His flat voice revealed

none of his disappointment that she continued to hearken back to him leaving as if it were a given and couldn't happen soon enough to suit her. "I told you. I'm not going anywhere."

Her eyes practically lit a fire beneath his skin as she glared at him. "I must know what your intentions are regarding Dorrie."

"I want to be a father to her."

"What kind of father?"

He steeled himself to hide his own doubts. "The best I can be." He thought of the way Dorrie's eyes brightened and how she called him da-da. It didn't matter that Anna said she called others the same. She would soon learn that Colby was *her* da-da.

"Do you think it's fair for her to think people can walk in and out of her life? Shouldn't she be able to trust people to be there for her through good times and bad?"

He slowly put his hammer down, crossed his arms over his chest and faced her squarely. "Say what you mean. That I left her when times were bad."

Anna nodded. "You did. You thought of no one but yourself."

It was the farthest thing from the truth but she didn't look to be in a very receptive mood for explanations. "It was the only way I knew to deal with Nora's death. I know you tried to tell me about

God's way but I couldn't see it. I couldn't believe it. I guess I wasn't ready. But I've changed. If you don't believe me then maybe you should at least give me a chance to prove it."

She stared at him.

"Anna, I thought you believed everyone deserves a chance. I recall how you used to say God didn't care where we came from, only whether or not we allow His love into our lives." He lowered his voice. "Don't you still believe it?"

"Of course I do. I just don't know if Dorrie should be the one you get to practice on. She needs security and the assurance those she loves will always do what's best for her."

"I'm not going to leave. But you're right about Dorrie. I don't want to upset her. She's obviously happy and well cared for." And disciplined in a way that was foreign to Colby. "I promise you, I won't take her away without your complete approval."

Anna's mouth fell open. She shook her head as if to clear her mind. "How can you make such a promise? You'll grow fond of her and want to take her when you leave. Or you'll marry—"

Her words might as well have been edged with razors they cut so deeply. Didn't she realize he'd only loved one woman in his whole life—her. He hadn't even loved Nora as he should. They'd married because they were both wanting someone who could share their problems.

He stopped her before she could go on. "Anna, I am not leaving again. Count on it."

A dark, haunted look filled her eyes. "I wish I could." She turned and fled before he could respond.

He stared after her for a long time. Truth was he didn't know what to say…or think. Her words gave him a sort of hopeless hope. As if she might care a bit about him but didn't want to.

He finally shook his head and returned to his work.

The pastor said to pray and so he did. *God, I've ruined so many things in my life. The good pastor says You will allow me to start over. I fear it's too late for me and Anna. But if You're like the pastor says and like I read in the scriptures, maybe You can change things. Make me into what I should be. Give me a chance to win Anna's love.*

Chapter Seven

Anna's thoughts went round and round, buzzing ceaselessly. He promised so much. To stay. To leave Dorrie with her.

None of it gave her any peace.

Suppertime approached and there were a hundred different details to attend to but her wayward emotions slowed her actions. She couldn't seem to catch up. And Alex needed reminding to do his work.

She found him playing with Dorrie in the front room. "Alex, run and do your chores now."

"Aww."

She ruffled his hair. "You have to do them so you might as well do them cheerfully."

But he scuffed the toes of his boots on the floor as he carried out the ashes. A few minutes later he rushed inside with the bucket of coal. "My chores are done. Can I go help Colby?"

Wonderful. Now Alex was falling under his spell, as well. He stood to be hurt and disappointed, too. But when had her brother ever been interested in anything to do with work?

She hesitated. It might do him good. As quickly as the thought came, she amended it. She couldn't encourage fondness between them. It wasn't worth the risk. Alex had endured enough losses already. "Maybe you should start your homework."

"I can do it after supper."

"Why don't you go outside and find someone to play with?" Persuading him to join in the play with other children was always a challenge. He preferred to stay in his room and read or play with Dorrie. She knew he needed companionship of others but she knew no way of making him seek it.

He sighed loudly and plunked down at the table. "You don't want me to go be with Colby."

"I guess I don't." At his disappointed expression, she felt she should explain. "Alex, I don't want you getting hurt."

Alex jutted out his chin. "How's helping him gonna hurt me?"

She could think of a hundred different ways, but she didn't want to get into a discussion when she knew Alex would demand explanations and details she didn't want to give him. "You just could, that's all." She turned away to prepare potatoes for supper.

"I guess I'll go outside," he murmured and dragged himself out the door with all the vigor of a man headed to the gallows.

Maybe she shouldn't have quelled his enthusiasm. It would do him good to work with a man for a change.

Her guilt lasted less than half a minute. She knew she'd done the right thing. Colby claimed to be changed but words came easy. She had no reason to trust him. It could be that about the time people began to count on him he'd toss it all over to disappear without a backward look. No, he had certainly given her no reason to trust him in the past nor in the present.

Supper was ready. Father, Alex and Colby would soon come in and sit down for the meal. Despite Colby saying he would leave Dorrie with her, she couldn't still the urge to hide the child. His assurances carried only as much weight as any promise from Colby had.

But Dorrie was hungry and would certainly fuss if confined to her room. Besides it was her duty to serve the meal. She had no choice but to put Dorrie in her high chair as Colby and Father came in.

Partway through the meal, Dorrie threw her food on the floor and wailed. "She's tired," Anna said, glad of a reason to take her from the table. As she prepared Dorrie for bed, the child fussed uncontrollably. "Poor baby." Sundays were always hard on her, upsetting her regular routine and Anna often paid for it on Monday. She wrapped Dorrie in her favorite blanket and rocked her until she fell asleep.

She returned to a kitchen now empty except for the remnants of the meal. Colby had left and Anna let out a heartfelt sigh of relief. Having Dorrie fuss had worked out rather well except for one thing— she was behind in her work. She should have the kitchen cleaned by now and be making sure Alex did his homework. She checked that he worked on his studies before she tackled the kitchen but she didn't disturb him to get his help with the dishes.

Finally she finished her chores. Dorrie was asleep. Alex in his room reading. Father had gone to visit. Anna felt the need for some fresh air and stepped into the yard, letting the warm evening wrap around her. A hauntingly, achingly beautiful tune filled the air. One of the hymns they'd sung on Sunday. She tipped her head toward the sound. Drawn by an invisible, melodic thread she followed it across the yard, past the ashes of the fire and in the back door of the church.

Colby sat on the front pew, his black-clad legs stretched straight out. He cupped his hands to his mouth playing a mouth organ. The sound encircled her. She'd only once before heard one played and that was for bouncy camp tunes. He played hymns, the pace much faster than one would sing, making the words dance through her head in a frenzy of joy.

He saw her and paused. "Am I bothering you?"

"No." She wasn't bothered so much as enticed to hear more. "I never heard you play one of those before."

"Something I picked up on my travels. I'm trying to learn the hymns you played."

"You're welcome to borrow one of the hymnals."

"Can't read music. I only hear it."

"Play some more."

His gaze stayed on her as he lowered his head and played the song that had drawn her over.

Something fragile as morning mist, soft as Dorrie's baby skin, hovered just outside her heart, reminding her of what they had once shared—how their hearts had beat to the same music, how their dreams had merged into one, how—

How he'd left.

She forced away the earlier feelings even though the action left her feeling lonesome.

He stopped before the end of the hymn. "I don't

recall the rest." He shifted his gaze toward the piano. "Would you mind playing it for me so I can learn it?"

Glad of something rational to do, she took her place on the bench.

"Play it all so I can be sure I got it right."

She began to play. Before she'd played two bars, he joined. She'd never made music with anyone else. Most times she couldn't even find someone to accompany her when she sang a solo in church. To have someone to share this love flooded her heart with joy and uncovered secret, lonely places she hadn't even known existed.

When he faltered, she played the ending over for him. He got it right immediately and sat back, grinning. "Thank you."

Her smile filled with pleasure. "I enjoyed it."

His gaze searched hers, looking deep into her heart, as if seeing things that had grown and developed since the last time they had been open and honest with each other.

She let her thoughts grow and expand, knew they filled her eyes even as they filled her heart. She was being more honest with him at this moment than she had been since his return.

They had often sat in this very building as she practiced the piano. She'd told him how she loved music and hoped someday to play as well as Rose.

Shyly she'd shared how the words and music spoke to her.

"Would you mind singing it as I play so I can hear the words inside my head?"

His voice seemed to come from a long tunnel, taking its time to reach her brain.

She jerked away and turned back to the piano keys. She must guard her heart. And thoughts. Hadn't she learned that lesson already?

So she played. He played. And she sang.

And despite her constant mental warnings, she let the music wash over her, numb her caution. She knew a height of pleasure so new and unfamiliar she didn't even know what to call it.

It was the music. That was all. Nothing more.

He stopped. "Wait. What was that last phrase?" He joined her on the piano bench so he could read the words himself.

She repeated the tune and they sang together. They finished the hymn. She paused, her hands in her lap. He grinned at her, his eyes sparkling with what she could only describe as pure, unfettered joy. Entangled in the music, she let his smile slip right past her reservations straight to her heart where it stirred together enjoyment and bliss into a surprisingly, delightful happiness. All the things that kept them at odds with each other vanished like dew in the morning sun. She allowed it.

Only because of how much she loved the music. Nothing more.

He flipped the pages of the hymnal. "Do you know this one?"

She chuckled. "I know all of them." She played it for him. Again they made music together. Song after song they played on, wrapped together in the melody and words, united in their enjoyment. She paused to turn the page.

"I remember when you said the songs were like God whispering in your heart. Now I know what you meant." His voice reverberated through her as if someone had struck the lowest key on the piano. At that moment, her defensive walls teetered.

Colby turned his attention back to the hymnal. "It's so dark I can hardly see the words anymore."

Anna looked around. The last golden rays of sun slanted through the window, sending bright lines across the pew, filling the rest of the room with shadows.

What was she thinking sitting here into the evening with this man? How could she consider trusting him again? Every time she thought he might be staying, he left. Every time she trusted him, he let her down.

She scooted off the bench. "I had no idea it was so late." No hiding the edginess in her voice.

"We were having too much fun."

She relented slightly at his quick smile. It wasn't his fault she'd let the music make her forget. "I enjoyed playing and singing together."

"I hope we can do it again."

At the invitation in his voice, she hesitated. In the fading light, she studied him. Who was he? Colby of her youth who shared the secrets of her heart? Or Colby of a year ago? Four years ago? Something hard and heavy lodged beneath her rib cage at the memory of being alone after Rose's death. The heaviness increased as her thoughts cleared. Only this moment did she realize she'd waited for his return, hoping and praying, only to have her heart scalded when he'd returned with a wife. He couldn't have made it any clearer that he did not share the feelings she had for him.

"I don't think that's wise. I must go." She scurried out the door, not slowing her steps until she slid into the silent kitchen. She padded into the front room. Father slept in his chair and she shook him awake. "It's time to go to bed."

He stirred. "I was waiting for you to come home."

"I was playing the piano." She often lost track of time as she practiced, but this time she hadn't been alone. Her cheeks stung with heat. What was she thinking to be with Colby all evening? She could imagine Mrs. Percy's comments if she knew. Thankfully there was no way she could.

She tiptoed in to check on Dorrie. The baby slept with her bottom in the air, a finger inserted in her mouth.

Anna clamped her hand to her lips to keep from crying out. Colby seemed changed—everything she'd always hoped he'd be—everything she knew he could be. She'd enjoyed his company more than she wanted to but the longer he hung about, the worse it would be for all of them. She couldn't see his presence being a cause for anything but disappointment and sorrow for Dorrie, though she guessed Dorrie was young enough to forget Colby when he left.

It was her heart that would be shattered yet again.

She doubted she'd survive the torture.

She hurried to her room and sat on the edge of her bed, her troubled thoughts tumbling around inside her head.

Lord, help me. Guide me to be wise. I don't want to be hurt again. I don't want Dorrie or Alex hurt. Oh, Lord. Help me. Protect me.

She knew God was all she needed but a great loneliness pushed at her insides until she feared it would consume her. Why had Colby come back? Why couldn't she simply forget him?

Chapter Eight

Anna worked at breakneck speed the next day as if she could outrace her troubled thoughts. She swept the floors until not even a hint of dust lingered. The mats had been shaken to within an inch of their lives. Every window ledge gleamed from a thorough washing. Even the stove had been blackened and polished. It was almost a shame to ruin the finish by cooking on it but knowing Mrs. Booker was still ill, she set a pot of soup to cook. Later in the morning, she poured the thick soup into jars and gave it to Father.

"Take it to the Bookers."

"This will be a real blessing to them. It will relieve her worries, too." He paused as if considering his words. "I'm sure you know what it's like when the woman of the house is ill or... Nothing has been the same since Rose died." With a resigned sigh, he left with the jars balanced in a shopping basket.

Her throat closed off so she couldn't bid him goodbye. She understood what he meant, yet it made her feel as if she could never measure up to Rose's standard. Not that she expected to.

Poor Father. He must be so lonely.

With a start, she realized she, too, was lonely. And despite her best efforts to pretend otherwise, her loneliness had a Colby shape to it.

Once they had discussed their dreams of families of their own. Anna always thought it was a shared dream—the two of them creating home and family together. She sighed. This was old business. He obviously didn't share the same hopes she did. She had learned to accept that and move forward.

Except his return had brought the dead dream back to life.

Only she and Dorrie remained at home and she spoke her thoughts aloud. "I'm so confused." The baby babbled away as excitedly as if Anna had promised her a trip to visit Laura. "And it's your father's fault. I don't know what to make of him."

Last night they'd spent two sweet hours playing and singing hymns together. At such times it was easy to forget her caution. To dream about the Colby who had once been her best friend, her confidant and the one she continued to hold close to her heart. But she didn't dare trust him.

She wanted to. She ached to. But she couldn't.

What did Colby really want? Why had he returned? Would he stay or leave again at the first hint of difficulty? And would he want to take Dorrie when he left?

She tried to reassure herself that he couldn't manage a baby girl on his own but it failed to still her doubts.

Anna scrubbed the soup pot with unusual vigor as her thoughts rocked back and forth between a renewed longing and too many uncertainties.

Father returned with news that Mrs. Booker sent her thanks for the soup. "She says her sister is coming to help while she regains her strength."

"That will be a blessing."

"Indeed." He went to his desk and pulled his Bible close.

Anna pressed her lips together. Father had never said Anna was a blessing for taking over after Rose's death.

She was only doing her duty and shouldn't expect praise for it but a word or two of acknowledgment would assure her she did a good job.

Enough feeling sorry for herself. God had given her a task and she would gladly do it, rejoicing she had the strength and ability.

She hummed as she returned to her work. It didn't pay to let her thoughts stray too far from God's goodness. Yet she wandered so often to the window, hoping for a glimpse of Colby that she began to wonder if she needed a tonic.

When Colby joined them for dinner, Anna could hardly look at him for fear he would see the confusion in her eyes. Why did she have this longing to be around him, to know he was nearby?

She must be overtired. And with well-honed self-discipline, she pushed cold hard steel into her thoughts.

She'd needed him before. Each time he had left. Now her life centered on Dorrie and Alex and running Father's house.

Dorrie went down for her nap and Father settled at his small desk in the front room. Since Colby had started repairs at the church, Father spent more time studying at home.

Anna looked at the pile of clothes to mend. She didn't want to tackle the job. She pulled out a bowl to mix a cake and put it back in the cupboard without measuring one ingredient. She heated some water and filled a basin, grabbed a couple of rags and washed the window behind the table. It gave her an unobstructed view of the church.

There was a time when her thoughts troubled her this way she would slip across and make her way to the front pew to sit and pray, her eyes open and focused on the cross. She always found what she needed—peace, wisdom, strength, courage....

She wished she could go to that place again, find what she needed.

She polished the glass slowly, not checking for streaks.

The cross no longer hung from the back wall. It leaned in the corner of the cloakroom. Perhaps she could slip in the front door without detection and recreate a special place of prayer near the cross. She needed so badly to feel God's assurance and direction right now.

She dropped the rag on the cupboard and hurried to the front room. "Father, I'm going out for a little while. Can you listen for Dorrie while I'm gone?"

Father waved acknowledgment without looking up from his notes.

She left the house through the front door and crossed to the church. Carefully she turned the knob and cracked the door only enough to allow her to duck through. She closed it soundlessly and tiptoed into the cloakroom. The cross leaned into the corner, so scarred and damaged she knew she would have to abandon hope of fixing it. No doubt someone would donate a new one. But for now she found comfort in this place of prayer—at the foot of an old rugged cross.

She sank to the floor facing it and let her thoughts roam freely until they grew quiet. Only then could she pray and bring her doubts and fears to God. *Lord, I feel like life is spinning out of control. I need Your wisdom.* She paused as more doubts and concerns sputtered to the surface. *I don't understand my feelings toward Colby. Part of me cares about him— has always cared about him. In fact—* Her thoughts stalled. *I have always loved him. But how is it possible when I'm not sure I trust him? Lord, I ask for You to give me a sign of what I should do.*

She heard a sound behind and glanced over her shoulder. Colby stood in the doorway.

"I heard something and thought I should investigate."

"I came here to think and pray."

"I won't interrupt then."

"I'm done." Though she had hoped God would speak in the stillness of her heart and she'd understand her feelings.

Colby crossed the small room in two strides and plunked down cross-legged on the floor beside her. "It means a lot to you, doesn't it?"

She knew he meant the cross. "It does."

Neither of them spoke but the silence was companionable.

Anna's heart filled with unutterable cries. "When Rose died I had to take over running the house and caring for Alex. I learned not to show my own grief in front of anyone. The only place I could acknowledge my sorrow was in the church. I would sit on the front pew, look at the cross and cry. I was so scared." She turned to confront him, doing her best to keep the accusation from her eyes as well as her voice. "I was so alone. I needed someone. Of course, I had God but I wanted more. Colby, where were you? Why did you leave?" She clamped her lips tight to stop the cry clinging to the tail end of her words.

Colby leaned closer. For a moment, she thought he meant to drape an arm across her shoulders, perhaps pull her against his heart where she wondered if she would find the release she longed for. And then he settled back. She told herself she wasn't disappointed but a part of her longed to bury her face against his chest and cry out the years of disappointment.

"Anna, I didn't think you would need me."

"How can you say that? I'd just lost Rose and baby Timmy. Suddenly I had to take Rose's place. How could you not realize how difficult it was for me? I thought we were friends."

"We were. I hope we still are."

"Friends don't abandon each other when things get tough."

Colby flinched. "How could I have helped?"

"By being here."

"You would have been disappointed in me. Besides, Rose's death hit me hard, too. She was like a mother to me."

They'd both been hurt by Rose's death and too young to know how to cope. Still… "I had to find my own way. Alone. I spent hours praying for wisdom and peace and strength to carry on." Her lips softened with the calm she reclaimed from that experience. "I found all I needed praying before this cross."

"You've managed very nicely."

"No thanks to you." She recalled another time she'd been frightened and uncertain how to face the task handed her. "Then you thrust Dorrie into my arms. I was so scared. I knew nothing about caring for a newborn. I used to come here when she was sleeping and beg God to guide me so I wouldn't kill her."

Colby jerked back. "Why would you think of killing her?"

She snorted at his shock. "I didn't *plan* to, but I feared I might make some colossal mistake. What if I fed her the wrong thing? What if she choked? What if she got sick and I didn't know how to treat her or, worse, didn't notice she was sick? The worries are endless."

He gave her a look of blue-eyed sympathy and something else—maybe regret. "I had no idea."

"Most of my worries were needless. I know that now. But at the time they seemed so real. So pressing. Only by trusting God could I face them."

"I'm here now. I'm not leaving."

At the moment she wasn't sure she wanted him to stay. She had too many unsettling doubts and fears. Too much to lose. And too much to forgive. Things too painful to even mention.

Colby sat there several minutes after Anna left. She'd had a lot to deal with but she'd coped. She'd done well. But she'd wanted him. Maybe even needed him. Why hadn't he stayed? Part of him wanted to. Why did he feel driven to leave whenever things got tough? What made him feel that was the best option for everyone? Not just him but Anna…and Dorrie.

He stared at the cross. Anna had come here often—only then the cross hung on the wall. She said she'd found answers. Would it work for him, too?

God, I feel like there is something bent in my life that pushes me to leave when I really want to stay.

Thoughts filtered through his brain. How much Rose's death had hurt. How he wanted to find comfort with Anna's family and maybe even do something to help them.

He tried to hear God speak but all he heard was his pa's voice. *What good are you, boy?*

Not that he put much pay on what Pa said. The old man wouldn't know a good thing if it reached up and grabbed him around the throat. As soon as Colby got big enough to realize he didn't have to take a whopping from him, as soon as he realized he could inflict as much pain as he took, he'd left, not wanting to start using his fists to equalize things between them.

Was that when it became easier to leave than to stay?

He shook his head. Somehow it didn't seem to fit. Walking away from his pa had been the right thing to do. It didn't have the same feel to it as leaving Steveville.

Nor did anything about Pa pull at him. But no matter how far he went, how fast he ran, and how deep into trouble he got, long invisible reins at the hand of an invisible, persistent, gentle driver pulled him back to Steveville.

And Anna.

"Man, you sure making a mess."

Colby turned from cutting away more damaged areas. "Slink, you old dog. Come on in." Slink had been one of his drinking buddies in the past.

Slink flashed a nervous smile and hung suspended in the doorway. "I ain't never been inside a church before. You think anybody would mind?"

"You're most welcome here. This is the place for sinners and the sick." Not everyone thought it but Pastor Caldwell said it was so and showed him a verse in the Bible to prove it.

Slink, always lean, had grown downright gaunt. "Looks like you could use a good feed."

"Don't eat much."

Colby guessed Slink likely lived on a liquid diet of cheap liquor. In fact, he clutched the neck of a bottle as he gingerly stepped into the sanctuary.

"That stuff is going to kill you."

"'Spect so." Slink looked at a pew as if he wanted to sit then changed his mind, a tight look around his mouth.

"Come on. Let's chew the fat."

Hesitantly, glancing up as if he expected a voice from heaven to order him to leave, Slink perched on the edge of a pew. His bottle tipped dangerously. "Heard you was back. Heard you wasn't drinking no more."

Colby took the bottle and set it upright on the bench then sat across from the man. "That's right. I've turned around with God's help and forgiveness." He explained how God accepted sinners.

"Yeah, but you ain't never been as bad as me." Slink looked miserable.

Little did the man know. Colby hoped no one would ever find out. He hadn't told the pastor all the details of his past. Pastor Caldwell had insisted he didn't need to know. It was between Colby and God, and the Almighty promised to wipe the slate clean. Colby figured if God said so it had to be true but he knew the shame of his deeds tinged his thoughts black. Expectation in Slink's expression told of his desire to hear more and Colby repeated what the pastor had said. "Nothing's too big nor too hard for God."

Hope laced with desperation on Slink's face.

Trying to recall Pastor Caldwell's words Colby explained the things God had done as best he could.

The back door opened, interrupting their discussion.

Anna strode in, pausing as her gaze lighted on Slink. "I didn't know you had company." Although she spoke softly Colby heard the unspoken criticism in her tone.

She shifted her gaze to the damaged wall. "It's going kind of slow, isn't it?"

Colby chuckled. "It will be done on time."

Slink scrambled to his feet, grabbed his bottle and shuffled toward escape.

"Come back anytime and we'll talk more," Colby called, then turned to Anna. His grin slid across his mouth, full of gladness at seeing her. Something happy bubbled behind his heart. "It's a fine day." Maybe they could sit and talk. It seemed they had almost found again that place of sweet agreement when their hearts had shared unspoken words.

She sniffed—a sound signaling displeasure, and grating up and down his spine.

He tensed, knowing whatever they gained talking before the cross had been taken back.

"I thought you'd be working."

He nodded as he slowly got to his feet. "I was. Took a break to talk to my friend." He didn't know why he felt he had to explain. Knew, too, how useless any excuses were when someone wanted to be mad at you and he knew, despite her quiet demeanor, that she was upset about something. Part of him said to back away, apologize, do whatever necessary to avoid fueling her anger but he'd stopped running from situations either physically or mentally. "Have I done something wrong?"

She blinked as if surprised at his directness. "Of course not." She stared again at the wall. "I can't help but worry a little. The work must be done in time for the celebration."

He knew there had to be more on her mind. "I know that already and it will be done. You can count on it."

Her nod seemed uncertain.

"Did you want to play the piano? I don't mind if you do. In fact, I'd kind of enjoy—"

"No. No. I wouldn't want to distract you from your work." She glanced over her shoulder. "Really I came to look at the cross again. I'm trying to figure out some way to redeem it." She headed toward the back.

He began to follow but she waved her hand. "I know where it is. Ignore me."

He hesitated. Seemed awfully clear she didn't want his company. And his disappointment was out of proportion. Yet he strained toward the cloakroom, aching to join her, recapture the few inches he thought they'd gained.

A few minutes later, she headed back down the aisle and out the door. "I won't bother you further."

He returned to fixing the wall, pounding in nails with two blows, finding release in the way his muscles burned.

Why had she gone over? What had she expected? Maybe to give him a chance to explain more about why he left and why he'd returned with a wife when she thought he loved her.

Instead she found him commiserating with a guy she'd only seen at a distance and even then the smell of booze almost knocked her off her feet. She'd seen the bottle on the bench. Had he been guzzling from it?

Changed indeed!

She fumed at her foolishness at hoping he had.

She fretted at how Colby could hurt Dorrie.

And she fussed about having to cook for the man.

But by the time Father came in for lunch, accompanied by Colby, she had her emotions firmly in hand. She would not allow her heart to rule her head. She would not allow herself to become a woman who couldn't see a man's falseness for the silly flutterings of her heart.

Colby smiled. "Hello."

Her control slid sideways. How could she feel this way about him if he was a scoundrel? How could he look so honest, meet her eyes with such calmness if he only pretended?

Alex slid in, out of breath from running from school. Father waited for him to settle in his chair then said grace. As he passed the biscuits and gravy, he said, "Mrs. Booker's sister arrived today."

Anna tried to gather her thoughts. "I should welcome her."

"That would be very nice."

There was nothing unusual about his announcing the arrival of visitors, nor of his expectation that she should be the official welcoming committee, yet there was something different about Father. Anna tried to get past her own heart turmoil to assess it but after studying him a moment decided she was mistaken.

As she turned to take the butter, her gaze collided with Colby's. He didn't say a word, didn't do anything more than look at her frankly, openly, but in that look she saw something that filled her with confusion—longing, promise, steadiness? Or was she only letting her own emotions fill her to over-brimming?

The whirlwind of confusion twisted through her as the day progressed, leaving her struggling to deal with the trials of the day. And there seemed to be a generous portion of them.

Dorrie didn't nap soundly and was irritable upon waking. At supper she didn't like the soup Anna served and threw her bowl on the floor. Anna scooped the screeching baby from her chair and carried her to the crib.

"Dorrie, you must stay here until you can stop screaming."

Shrieks followed her back to the kitchen where she cleaned up the mess.

"Anything I can do to help?" Colby asked softly.

His gentle tone almost proved her undoing. She stiffened her spine to keep from wailing and saying, *Yes, you can hold me. You can handle Dorrie's temper tantrum.*

Father answered Colby's question. "Dorrie exhibits a defiant attitude at times. I've found it's best to leave Anna to deal with it."

Out of sight as she scrubbed the floor, Anna rolled her eyes. Since Rose's death Father left the discipline of Alex to Anna. Before that Rose ran the house with order and control. After Dorrie came, it was one more responsibility for Anna, one Father never seemed to notice. Not that she minded. She loved Dorrie like she hadn't thought possible after watching Rose and Timmy die. In fact, she sat back on her heels momentarily as she considered the revelation, loving Dorrie healed some of the hollowness Anna carried inside her heart after the accident robbed her of her stepmother and baby brother.

She finished cleaning the mess and dumped out the dirty water. She returned to the table but her own food had grown cold and held no appeal as she listened to Dorrie crying.

Colby squeezed her shoulder as he left the table. "Do you want me to talk to her? She might listen to me." He lowered his voice to a growl. "I can sound quite menacing if I try."

She suddenly felt better. She'd gladly let someone else tackle Dorrie in her present state. "Go ahead. See what you can do."

As he went to Dorrie's room, Anna strained to catch what he said. She couldn't hear his words but his voice rumbled, not growly and menacing but calming. Dorrie shuddered a sob or two and grew quiet. Colby talked on for a few minutes. Anna caught only a word or two. Not enough to know what transpired.

She stared as Colby returned, a sobered Dorrie in his arms.

"Dorrie has something to say to you." He smiled encouragement at his daughter.

"I sorry, Mama." At the catch in Dorrie's throat, Anna's heart almost melted from her chest. She jerked to her feet and kissed Dorrie's cheek.

"I forgive you, sweetie." She lifted her gaze and realized how close she was to Colby, close enough to see the silvery flecks in his irises, to see the warmth in his gaze and feel the endless connection between them that had never quite been quenched. It promised endless sunshine.

They'd once shared so many things—from the games they enjoyed to their secret thoughts. And recently they'd shared a love of music and an unspoken love of this child. But it wasn't enough.

She turned and gathered dishes from the table. For the space of a heartbeat she thought of speaking to Father about her worries but he'd only say a person had to accept people at face value. He despised suspicions and mistrust between people. He would not understand Anna's need for caution.

But she must be careful. If Colby broke her heart once again she might never recover. She must be strong, not only for her sake, but for Dorrie's, too. As well as for Alex and Father.

Colby held Dorrie a few minutes longer then set her down. Anna allowed herself a quick glance at him. His smile flooded with love and longing as he watched Dorrie. He looked up, met Anna's eyes. She felt his expectation, his silent pleading but she couldn't give the response he sought. The walls she'd constructed around her heart prevented it. As did her experience.

His eyes filled with dark regret. "I best get to work." He grabbed his hat and rushed outside.

Anna watched long after he'd disappeared from sight, unable to conquer a wish that they could go back in time.

It was impossible to recapture what they'd had. Yet... Her heart swelled with "what-ifs" and "if onlys."

Enough.

She grabbed dishes and plunged them into hot water, scouring them so hard it surprised her she didn't break something. Her efforts did nothing to ease the storm raging within her heart.

Later, after Alex returned from school, Anna mixed up a cake. She checked the oven. It wasn't hot enough. She reached for the coal pail. Empty. Alex's after-school chores included filling it.

"Alex?"

He didn't answer. Where had he gone?

Chapter Nine

Anna checked each room in the house, calling her brother's name but didn't find him. Where was he? He never wandered away without letting her know. Finally she glanced out the window what she saw made her knees buckle. She grabbed the cupboard for support and sucked in a gulp of air that stuck partway to her lungs. Ignoring her shaky limbs, she raced out the door. "Alex, get down from there this very instant." She paused, picturing him coming from the roof in a tumbling fall. "Use the ladder and be careful."

Alex lifted his head but other than that made no move toward obeying. "I'm helping Colby pull off the burned shingles."

"I don't want you on the roof. You might fall."

"He's perfectly safe." Colby's look was steady, reassuring.

But she was not reassured and sent him a glare meant to scald him. "How dare you put him at risk."

Colby's gaze remained steady, solid. "I wouldn't."

She pressed her palm to her chest, massaging the tightness that refused to let go. "He might get hurt."

"Anna, believe me, I wouldn't let that happen."

She desperately sucked in air, which did nothing to relieve the tension in her chest. "You can't guarantee that. No one can. Accidents happen. It's best not to take chances."

He studied her with unblinking concentration, his gaze going on and on, past the brittleness stinging in her eyes, straight toward the fear surrounding her soul.

She averted her eyes, afraid of exposure, and looked at Alex but couldn't bear the sight of him perched so nonchalantly on the roof. Instead, she glanced at the bare studs of the back wall. A shiver raced across her shoulders. So many things could happen—accidents, fires—

"Are you planning to wrap him in cotton wool and keep him so close he can't breathe just to make sure he doesn't face risks?" Colby had come down from the roof and stood two feet away. He kept his voice low, meant for her ears only.

"What do you know about dealing with bad

things? Seems to me you drown your sorrows so you can't feel or else you run. I don't have those sort of options nor would I take them if I did." She gasped at the accusations she had spewed at him. "I'm sorry. I should not have spoken so hastily."

"You spoke the truth. I don't deny it." His voice was harsh as if he wished he could. "But I'm back. To stay." He lowered his voice. "But we were talking about Alex. Anna, you can't protect him from life. You need to let him grow up."

"He's only fourteen." Even as she spoke she knew Alex should be more mature than he was. But she didn't know how she could make him grow up. Didn't it happen in its own good time?

"I was on my own by his age."

"He has nothing to make him run away from home."

"I appreciate that."

She nodded and turned to again order Alex from the roof.

Colby touched her shoulder, causing every nerve in her body to tremble. "Anna, what about your faith? Doesn't it teach you to trust God with the things that come into our lives?"

Red-hot flashes burst across her eyesight. She blinked, fearing another fire but the flames were inside her and posed no threat to anyone but Colby. "How dare you lecture me on faith?"

His eyes turned stormy-blue. "I am not lecturing, merely pointing out that life involves risks and faith should make us able to face them without fear."

The truth of his words drilled through her head. Her faith should be stronger. Her faith was her only defense. If she neglected to honor it, what protection did she have from disaster? "You're right, of course. I must trust God to take care of me and those I love."

He nodded, his eyes still filled with uncertainty as if he expected something different from her.

"Like I told you, He sustained me through the loss of Rose and Timmy. He upheld me when you—" She stopped. She would not confess how her world had crashed when he came back with a wife. Or when he'd left again. He must never know that she still loved him in some forbidden corner of her heart that she had barricaded.

"When I what?"

She avoided meeting his gaze, afraid he would read the truth in her eyes—her pain, her love. "You left me to raise Dorrie."

"It was the best thing I could do at the time. I wasn't ready to be a father."

If he meant that to give her reassurance…

Did he think he was ready to father Dorrie now? And if so, where did that leave Anna?

But she couldn't deal with the possibility he might take her away, and she forced her thoughts back to Alex.

Colby struggled with his feelings. Was he ready to be a father now? This afternoon he had successfully dealt with Dorrie in a gentle manner even though she kicked and screamed when he approached her. He had not resorted to his father's methods. It felt good. And right. But it was only one time. Could he do it day in and day out?

He didn't know. But he knew one thing. He was through with running. He intended to stay right here and be as involved in Dorrie's life as he could without putting her at risk.

In the meantime, he had a church to repair.

He glanced toward Alex who continued to pull out damaged shingles, oblivious to the drama on the ground below him. The boy—almost man—needed to cut the apron strings both he and his sister clung to. "What about Alex?"

By the way her eyes darkened and narrowed, he knew she struggled with her need to keep Alex safe and her desire to prove she had enough faith.

How much faith was enough? He didn't know. It was a question he'd have to ask Pastor Caldwell.

Fear and caution seemed about to win the battle in her mind. "I don't want him on the roof.

It's too dangerous." She called Alex and again told him to get down.

Alex glanced at Colby, seeming to want his approval.

"How about you burn the lot?" Colby said.

"Sure."

Colby felt Anna gasp as Alex scampered down the ladder to grab the wheelbarrow and race it over to the smoldering pile. The flames lick higher as he tossed on bits of wood.

She pressed her palm against her breastbone as she watched the flames. "I will never see a fire without remembering the fear of seeing homes engulfed and waiting, praying, fully expecting to see our home go." She swallowed hard.

Colby ached to comfort her. He thought of pulling her into his arms and holding her until her fears subsided, but she stiffened if he so much as brushed her hand. Yet his need to help her could scarcely be bottled up. "I heard how the good Lord spared the church and your house." He bravely touched her elbow. "Seems God protected you."

She turned her gaze to him, the flames still flickering in her irises. "But why us and not the others?"

He tried to think of an answer but he was no preacher and he was distracted by the warmth of her arm beneath the fabric of her sleeve, and even more than that—the way his blood gathered up the glow where they connected and fired it all the way to his heart to throw fresh fuel on the flame of their past. He wanted to rekindle what they had once had.

Or did he want to take the embers from the past and start something new? The latter, he realized with all his heart. Something new, something fresh and powerful. *Please God, give me another chance.*

But how many chances did God give a person? Colby knew he'd had more than his fair share. Making it back to Steveville without detection or interference might have used up the last of his chances. He pushed his thoughts back to the subject at hand.

"He'll be careful. I'll make sure of it."

She held his gaze. Slowly, her eyes cleared and her fears seemed to subside.

He smiled, relieved she chose to trust him with her little brother. Given time, perhaps he could prove she could trust him with her heart.

A little later, he hurried over for supper, eager to see if anything between them had changed, if the tiny crack he'd seen had widened.

Dorrie babbled a greeting when Colby walked into the kitchen. She waved her hands as she talked and pointed toward the table.

"Sorry, little gal. I don't understand you." Apart from the sweet words of da-da.

Anna picked up Dorrie and settled her in the

high chair. "We don't understand most of what she says, either." The smile she gave Dorrie trembled when she glanced at Colby.

He sensed her hesitation, as if she couldn't decide if their feelings should be allowed to progress or not. He smiled. He had all the time in the world to prove she could trust him.

She served the meal then toyed with her very tasty brown beans and corn bread as if they had no more flavor than chalk.

"These are delicious, Anna. You're an excellent cook."

She looked at him then, her eyes wide as if his words surprised her. And he saw something more, a flash of pleasure at his praise. Her eyes brightened. Her mouth curved sweetly. "Thank you." Her gaze lingered no longer than a heartbeat but in that brief encounter he saw something he cherished—an acknowledgment of something warm and sweet between them.

He grinned, happy he'd managed to bring a smile to her lips. Even happier because of what he'd seen—she felt something toward him though she might not be willing to admit it yet.

He enjoyed the rest of the meal even though Anna's gaze darted away from him each time he looked her direction. Her actions only made it plainer that she had feelings for him but they frightened her. He silently promised he'd never again give her reason to fear opening her heart to him.

In the next few days, Alex found excuses to check on Colby and offer help if the work interested him. He sauntered over again as Colby prepared pieces of lumber to fix the roof. "Whatcha' doing?"

Colby explained how he had to repair the structure. "Want to help?"

Alex gave the lengths of lumber a dubious look. "Is it hard?"

"I wouldn't think it would be for a boy your size." He'd already noticed Alex avoided anything challenging. "Besides, hard work builds muscles." He had his sleeves rolled past his elbows. He shoved one higher and flexed his biceps to show Alex. "I've been working hard since I was twelve. And it hasn't done me any harm. Isn't that about your age?"

Alex shoved his hands behind his back as if ashamed of his lack of muscle. "I'm fourteen."

"Only one way to get muscles—build 'em with use."

Alex hesitated about ten seconds. "What do you want me to do?"

"I'm going up the ladder. You hand me these one at a time." It wasn't hard work. A six-year-old could handle most of it. "It will save me a pile of time not having to run up and down."

Alex did as Colby suggested. When the boards were all up top, Alex climbed the ladder and started to join him.

"I don't think Anna wants you up here."

"Yeah, she'll get mad if I get on the roof."

"Anna gets mad?" Did she still struggle with a temper that made her slam doors? "I don't believe it." She always seemed so calm and in control. "What does she do?"

"She tweaks my ear."

Colby choked back a laugh at the injured tone in Alex's voice. Little did he know how innocent a tweak on the ear sounded to Colby and what a mercy that was the worst Alex experienced.

Until he'd found his way to this family he had no idea how gentle life could be. He'd wanted a share of it. Had found it for a time. He'd left for what he figured were pretty good reasons. But no matter how far he went, how bad he was, how hard he drank, how loud he roared, he could never get away from wanting that sort of family, and the belonging he'd experienced nowhere else but here. Even if Anna never let him back into her life, at least Dorrie was in the sort of family he ached for. He consoled himself with that fact. "You can hand me nails as I need them."

He and Alex worked in companionable silence as he nailed the new pieces into place.

A door opened and closed next door.

Alex groaned. "I forgot I'm supposed to be getting Anna coal."

"Run along and do it. And if you've caused her any inconvenience, the manly thing would be to apologize."

"I will." He raced off to the coal shed.

Colby returned his attention to roof repairs. Suddenly he got the feeling someone watched him. He sat back to check the surroundings and stared straight into Anna's face—just inches away at the edge of the roof. His heart burned up his throat and he reached to steady the ladder. "You shouldn't be up here."

"Why not? Didn't you say it was perfectly safe?"

"Yes. No." For a man. Not a woman. Especially not a woman who owned a large portion of his heart.

The past few days there existed a tension between them—a not unpleasant sense of anticipation, as if things were about to change.

He prayed it was so.

"Are you here to help?" He sounded as doubtful as he felt. This was not her work. She had her hands more than full running her father's home. That gave him pause. Would she ever be able to leave? What would happen to Alex if she did? He chomped down hard, not liking the questions he'd raised.

She laughed. "I don't think you need my kind of help. No, I'm here to thank you."

"For what?"

"For what you're doing with Alex."

He shuffled about to sit cross-legged so he could face her and sought for the right words to say. A few days ago, she didn't want Alex helping him, feared he might come to harm. But in that short time, she'd changed her mind. Now she was grateful. It was a bigger beginning than he could have thought possible. "Anna, I don't deny I've given you plenty of reason to doubt me in the past. But I vow by everything I care about that I've changed." It wasn't only his determination that made his words true. It was what God was doing. "You can trust me. You can trust God to help me." His voice grew deeper as he risked speaking his desires. "You and I could be friends again."

Caution darkened her eyes.

His chest tightened as though someone squeezed him hard. He shouldn't have said anything. It was too soon.

She tipped her head, squinting against the brightness and searched his gaze. Some hair had fallen from her usual roll and the breeze tugged it across her cheeks.

Resisting an urge to capture the wayward strands and tuck them behind her ear, Colby held still, let her delve deep into the peaks and valleys and secret places of his soul.

With a deep sigh, she lowered her eyes.

He felt both seared by a hot sun and watered by a gentle rain.

"We'll see." She started down the ladder and paused. "Again, thanks for helping Alex."

Anna's thoughts tangled inside her head.

How could they be friends if she didn't trust him? A portion of her wanted to. Another portion warned her to remember his past. What did she want to believe?

She heard the answer deep inside her and it frightened her. She wanted to believe he was different. She wanted to believe he planned to be part of Dorrie's life. A part of hers. Knowing she could so easily switch back and forth from mistrusting Colby to actually enjoying his company and wanting to be friends, caused Anna to lose an hour or more of sleep.

Pain grabbed her heart in a cruel fist and gave it a vicious twist as she remembered watching Rose and baby Timmy die. In that moment she knew she would never again let herself care about someone who might be snatched from her, or who might leave her like Colby had a habit of doing.

If only she could discuss her problems with

Rose. But she hadn't had that privilege in four years. She gave a frustrated sound—half sigh, half moan. How could she be so confused?

Next morning, as soon as she finished cleaning the kitchen, she told Father, "I'm going to visit Laura." She had to talk to someone. Perhaps Laura would have some good advice. After all she was now a married woman with children of her own.

Over tea, she and Laura discussed how baby Gloria had grown. "She slept through the night Saturday."

"Seems only yesterday Dorrie was that small." Her fears and worries rushed from their hiding spot in the back of her mind where she pushed them daily and tried to pretend they didn't exist. "Laura, what will I do if Colby tries to get her back?" It wasn't the subject she really wanted to discuss but she feared talk about her mixed-up feelings for Colby would only make Laura think she was weak and fickle.

"Is that what he wants?"

"He said I was doing a good job of raising her. He *said* he didn't intend to take her away." Unless Anna gave her full approval and she couldn't see that happening. She loved the child as her own.

"You don't believe him?" Laura rocked baby Gloria as they talked.

Anna turned her teacup round and round and tried to find words to express her tangled thoughts.

"I want to believe him. But I don't know what to think."

"Anna, what's really bothering you?"

"I…I can't seem to decide what to think of him. Sometimes I want to believe he is as good as he seems." Slowly, hesitantly, her feelings almost too fragile to voice, she told how he worked with Alex and how he'd helped with Dorrie. "We have even enjoyed playing music together but—"

"What worries you?"

"I don't want to start trusting him only to have him walk away again."

Laura paused to lay the baby in her cradle. She refilled their teacups and took her seat again before she answered. "Anna, are you beginning to care for Colby in a special way? Is that what frightens you?"

"I—" She gulped as her mind stung with so many things she didn't want to face—her need for more than what she had, her fears at things changing. She was comfortable with who she was, what she had. She liked her security. She wanted to give the same security to Dorrie. "I don't want anything to change."

Laura smiled. "Anna, things must change. Alex is almost grown. He'll be wanting to do things away from home soon."

Anna thought of how eager her brother seemed to

help Colby. Was it only the beginning of Alex leaving?

She didn't want to think about it. If she could she would pull Alex close and keep him there.

"Dorrie will go to school. And before you know it, she'll be wanting to marry and start her own family."

Anna chuckled looking at Dorrie babbling away as she played with a doll Laura gave her. "She can barely walk and her vocabulary is limited to half a dozen words. I hope she isn't thinking marriage already."

Laura laughed, too. "Not yet, of course, and hopefully not for a long time but my point is things are going to change whether you want them to or not."

"I wish they wouldn't."

"But life can't stand still. Anna, my dear friend, I have known you a long time. I've watched you cope with tragedies and challenges that would knock most of us to the ground. But it seems to me that you've wrapped life around you in a tight little ball. Isn't it time you let go and let God bring something new into your life?"

Anna squeezed her hands into fists. The idea of change frightened her. In her experience change hadn't proven to be a good thing. "I don't think I can handle it."

Laura laughed until her eyes watered. "I'm sorry," she finally managed to get out between chuckles. "This from a young woman who has handled more in the past few years than most of us handle in a lifetime, God willing."

"I only did what I had to do." Shaking with uncertainty and doubting her ability every step of the way. "And only with God's help."

"Will God help any less in the future?"

Laura's soft words smoothed Anna's concerns. "It would be different if I knew I could truly trust Colby."

"I wish it weren't so but people can't always be trusted. All I can say is take your time. Be cautious. And trust God to show you the way."

As Anna returned home she thought of Laura's advice. *Take your time. Trust God. Be cautious.*

Did that mean she should avoid Colby? Or explore their relationship? She didn't know but when Father handed her the list of hymns at supper, a thrill of expectation raced through her and she stole a look at Colby. "I'll practice them tonight," she murmured. Neither of them needed to speak to know they would play the hymns together.

As soon as Dorrie was asleep, she slipped over to the church. The room was warm from the afternoon sun. Dust drifted in the air accompanied by the cedar scent of newly sawn lumber. She didn't see Colby and could not deny the way her heart dipped with disappointment.

Chapter Ten

Colby heard her enter as he sat cross-legged in front of the cross where he'd been for some time, thinking and praying. He could understand why Anna felt the cross was so special. He, too, found it easier to direct his thoughts heavenward as he sat there.

"Anna, I'm in here." He waited for her to join him, sensing a calmness in this place that made it easier to speak honestly without fears and doubts getting in the way.

He turned as she slipped into the room and at the eager look on her face, his heart took off like a wild horse. He wondered it didn't leap from his chest. She cared. Lifting a hand he reached for her. "Come and sit beside me."

She hesitated only fractionally before she took

his hand and let him draw her to his side. She sat close enough he barely had to shift for their shoulders to brush. When she didn't make any effort to move, his heart settled into a steady gallop.

"I was sitting here praying. And remembering."

"Remembering? What sort of things."

A smile started deep in his heart and slowly spread to his lips, rounding his cheeks and filling his eyes. "You and me."

She lowered her head and studied her hands curled in her lap.

He felt her uncertainty as forcefully as if she'd pressed her palms to his chest and held him at bay. But there were things that needed to be said, things worth keeping despite all that had come after. "Remember the first time you baked bread?"

Her head came up then, surprise swathing her features. And then she whooped with laughter. "That's your top memory? What a disaster. I had to bury it in the garden."

He chuckled. "Several weeks later the Kleins' dog dug it up and dragged it all over town. No one could figure out what he had."

"Rose knew but she never let on."

"It was a lot of fun."

"More like embarrassing. Do you know how I dreaded that someone would figure out what it was and that I was responsible?"

He reached for her hand. Again, she let him. He examined her long fingers, turned the palms upward to see little scars where she'd nicked herself with a knife and hard little calluses at the base of each finger—evidence of how hard she worked.

The air between them was fragile with hopes and expectations.

Slowly she withdrew her hand. "Colby, what brought you back?"

Her whispered words strummed through his heart. He ached to tell her the whole truth but he couldn't.

If she knew…

If anyone found out…

"I didn't like what I was becoming."

"What?"

"My old man."

Something flared in her eyes. Something he took for compassion, maybe even hope. And she claimed his hand, gently squeezing it.

Her touch raced straight to his heart and grabbed it.

"Is that why you run? Because you think you'll be like your father?"

He rubbed his thumb across her knuckles as he studied their joined hands and considered her question. Why did he leave when Rose died? What was he afraid of? Why did he leave again when Nora died? What filled his heart with such dread that he had jumped on his horse and rode straight into the jaws of trouble in the hopes of cauterizing his thoughts?

Anna waited patiently, insistently. She deserved some sort of answer even if he didn't have one.

"I knew I couldn't be what you needed."

She gave his hand a brisk shake. "What did you think I needed?"

He didn't know. He shrugged.

"So what's different now?"

The question caught him squarely between the eyes and he grunted. Had anything changed? Had he changed? "Maybe nothing. I only know I'm through running."

She studied him for a long moment, looking past his words, past his own doubts and questions, straight to the depths of his heart.

He hardly dared breathe as he faltered between letting her see all his secret inner places and the need to shelter them. Slowly, under her intense study, he opened himself to her, all except for one corner, which he barred behind thick doors.

She must never know.

Finally, she nodded as if satisfied. "God's hand has been on you since the first day you rode into Steveville."

Yes. She accepted he was changed, that he was

through running. He wanted to leap up and shout to the heavens his joy. Instead he grinned until his ears wriggled in protest.

She pushed to her feet. "I need to practice the hymns."

"Mind if I join you?"

The look she sent over her shoulder gave him even more joy. "Hoped you would."

Colby smiled as he measured boards to fit the wall. Playing music with Anna last night had been especially happy as they shared a new understanding. He felt as if she had opened her heart and welcomed him. Just a bit. Still tenuous. But progress.

He heard a shuffling in the entryway and went to investigate. He found Slink and Luke, another old buddy. Luke had obviously tried to polish his appearance. His old woolen pants had been brushed until only a few flecks of straw remained. He'd slicked back his hair and tried to shave though from the number of nicks Colby guessed he needed to sharpen his razor. Or steady his hand. He twisted a battered bowler hat in his fingers.

"Slink here said you know something about God."

"I tried to tell him what you said but I got it all mixed up." Slink's face wrinkled in concern.

"So we thought best we come and ask you to tell us."

"Glad to." He led the men inside and explained what he knew.

A blast of sunlight filled the room as the back door opened. Facing the glare he couldn't make out who stood in the doorway.

Then the door clicked closed and Anna stood blinking as her eyes adjusted to the dimmer interior. "Colby?"

His heart did a rat-ta-tat against his ribs at the sound of his name on her lips. "Over here."

She walked toward him, saw his friends and hesitated. "You've got…company."

"My friends Slink and Luke. Miss Caldwell," he said to the men. Slink had already jerked to his feet and backed away but Luke rose and nodded formally.

"Pleased to make your acquaintance, ma'am."

Anna tipped her head in acknowledgment but retreated so fast Colby wondered she didn't trip and fall on her rear.

"Did you want something?" he called after her.

"No. Nothing." She ducked out so quickly he could almost believe she'd never been there.

He stared at the dark wood of the door. What had she wanted? Maybe only to spend time with him. The idea filled him with sweet hope.

Slink wouldn't stay after that.

Colby went to the door with the men. "Feel free to come back anytime."

* * *

Anna watched out the window as evening shadows pooled between the house and church. She knew she had turned into a spy, but she couldn't help it. The first time she'd discovered those strange men dropping into the church, she'd been shocked, dismayed even. But when it continued day after day, she grew suspicious. These were the friends she'd seen Colby with after his wife died. Drunk and disorderly for the most part.

Could he be toying with the idea of leaving again?

She hated to be suspicious of him. Especially when every day she found something more she liked about the man.

She liked the way he seemed to know how to play with Dorrie—gentle but not babyish stuff. Even though Dorrie's speech was little more than a babble she understood what was said to her. He talked to the child with real words.

The other day he brought her a little puzzle he'd made from wood scraps. Anna wanted to say Dorrie was far too young for such games but she held her tongue and waited to see how he would handle his child.

"Look, Dorrie. A puzzle."

Dorrie babbled excitedly.

Anna laughed. "A whole paragraph that we don't understand."

Colby grinned. "I know what she said. She said, 'Thanks, Da-da. It's the best puzzle I ever got. Now show me how to make it.'"

Anna shook her head. "Seems you both have a good imagination."

"We understand each other."

A quiver of fear trembled through Anna. She suppressed a desire to grab Dorrie, whisk her into the bedroom and lock the door behind them.

Colby's presence threatened Dorrie's security even more than it threatened Anna's.

She did not want either of them to be hurt.

"That's my girl."

His words pulled Anna from her thoughts. Under his supervision, Dorrie had pushed together the few puzzle pieces. He seemed as pleased as she was at her success.

Colby's head bent close to Dorrie's. Dorrie's hair was lighter but no doubt would darken to the same color as Colby's. They looked at each other, grinning widely, and Anna could not deny the similarity in their facial features any more than she could deny that Dorrie thrived with Colby's attention.

So did Alex. He seemed to have grown six inches and gained a self-confident stride after helping Colby with the church repairs. She liked the way he had managed to get Alex to hold his head up and speak directly to him.

Take your time. Be cautious.

Anna had turned away, pretending to be busy at the stove. Was it too late to be cautious? She couldn't deny she liked the way he smiled so readily and laughed so often. Seems her heart had gone it's own way.

She liked sharing her love of music with someone—someone whose eyes flashed blue depths when their gazes connected.

How could she feel this way toward him and yet still be full of suspicion? One day she felt close to him as if they had recaptured the earlier days of their relationship. The next moment she knotted up with fear and mistrust. She trusted God. Colby insisted that meant trusting God was working in his life. Could she do both? She didn't know.

On top of that, she worried what his presence meant to her role as Dorrie's mama.

She tightened her lips. Her own security felt a little shaky, too, when she considered her reactions to the man.

Anna had vowed to stay away from the church when he was working but to be completely honest, she'd hoped for another satisfying evening of music with Colby.

Instead, she watched as two pairs of tough-looking men slipped into the church. She glanced

over her shoulder, wondering if she should alert
Father, then she dismissed the idea completely.
Father would say the church was open to the public.
Anyone was welcome to go in and pray and med-
itate.

But were they doing that? Or tempting Colby to
his old way of life?

She sighed heavily. Suspicion and selfish longing for a repeat of the kind of connection she'd felt
a few nights ago twisted like sheets left too long
on the clothesline. How was it possible to feel such
conflicting emotions at the same time?

She turned from the window. But almost immediately returned to it. If those men left soon she
could still hurry over before Colby departed.

As if her thoughts had prodded them, the men
crowded out the front door, paused to speak to
Colby again then shuffled down the sidewalk
talking together.

She waited until they were out of sight.

Suddenly she didn't care about music. She
wanted to find out what was going on with those
men. "I'm going to the church," she called to Father
and rushed across the yard.

Before she reached the door, she heard the sound
of Colby playing the mouth organ and faltered as
her heart and mind warred with one another. Pushing aside the way the music filled her with mem-

ories of shared pleasures, she cranked her spine into stiff attention and marched into the building.

Colby stopped playing and grinned at her.

She cranked her spine a notch firmer. Not even his smile of welcome must be allowed to divert her. "Colby, what were those men doing here?"

He slowly lowered his hands to his lap as his smile fled. "You object?"

"Depends on why they're here."

"You think they're up to no good?"

She waggled her hands. "Is it so hard to just tell me?"

He shrugged. "Seems to me you're judging without cause."

"I just want to know."

"When are you going to learn to trust me?"

Trust. *Dear God, how I want to. And yet how afraid I am he's going to leave again.* She narrowed her eyes and stared hard at him, revealing nothing of her errant feelings. "When I can be sure it's safe to."

He nodded slowly and repeatedly. "You mean when you can be sure there are no risks. Well, I can't promise you that. No one can. Did Rose promise she would be here forever? She didn't have a say in it, did she?"

Pain spun through her and erupted in a cry. "How dare you compare yourself with Rose?"

"I'm not. But isn't that where our suspicions and failures started?"

"You left. That's where they began."

"I'm sorry. I had nothing to offer you."

"All I wanted was someone to hold my hand. Be my friend." The ache she'd denied since he'd left consumed her. It swept away reason and caution in its relentless invasion. "I waited for you to come. Then I waited for you to come back. When you did, you brought a wife." It took the last trembling remnants of her self-control to clamp her mouth shut so she wouldn't say more.

He stared past her. "I thought you knew."

"What?"

"I didn't love her."

She gasped. "What a dreadful thing to say."

"She knew it. We didn't marry out of love."

"Then why?"

"Because we found comfort in sharing our circumstances. She was under the guardianship of an uncle who confined her to the back room and worked her like a mule." Slowly he brought his gaze back to her and she read the pain, the confusion, the desperation that almost made her cry out again. "Besides, don't you see? It was the ultimate form of running away."

Pain scorched every breath, every pore of her that he would marry someone he didn't love to what—escape her? "Why?" she whispered. "Why did you have to protect yourself against me?"

"It wasn't you. It was me."

"I don't understand."

"Me, either. But all I can say is I've reached the end of my running. I am back to stay."

His words promised things she wanted but they barely scratched the surface of her defensiveness. He said it was because of him but it was her that had been hurt. She could not comprehend.

"I was afraid of disappointing you. Failing you."

"You keep saying that as if I had somehow put unreal expectations on you. If I did, I'm sorry."

"You didn't. Like I said. It wasn't anything to do with you."

"And what happened to this thing that sent you running? This thing you don't seem able to identify?"

"Maybe I outran it."

"What? What is *it?* And what if it catches up to you again?" Why couldn't he give a straight answer? Though if he said she was *it,* that might prove more than she could handle.

He took her hands and faced her squarely.

She wanted to pull away but his look held her like a freshly spun spiderweb made with steel threads.

"I don't know why I ran. Maybe I will never

understand. But this one thing I do know, forgetting what is behind and reaching for those things that are better. I press toward the mark for the prize of the high calling of God in Christ Jesus. That's from Philippians, Chapter 3. Your father explained it was like running a race. If I look over my shoulder I'm slowed down. I might get off course or even stumble. I'm not looking back. I'm not going back. The only direction I'm running is straight for the prize of the high calling of God."

Her mouth dropped open. She blinked. This was not the Colby she remembered—uncertain of who he was, what he was. "You're different."

He grinned as he squeezed her hands and pulled her so close they were almost nose to nose. "You're finally getting it."

She jerked back, stunned by his words, even more stunned by his assurance.

"Isn't it about time you started to accept me?"

"I—" She couldn't finish. This was what she wanted. This closeness. This assurance. Yet— "Those men?"

He sighed and pulled away. "I can see it's going to take some time. Those men are the ones I used to drink with. They've come to hear about God. You see, I told them I was changed…." He let his words trail off.

But she understood what he didn't say…his

former drinking buddies were more ready to believe him than she.

"I'm afraid," she whispered.

"Of me?"

"Of being hurt, disappointed." She tore her gaze from him, but felt more lonely than ever and slowly shifted until she met his eyes again.

He nodded. "Anna, there are no guarantees in life. I can't give you any. No one can. But you can't pull life around you like a blanket and hope that you can somehow prevent anything unpleasant."

Hadn't Laura warned her things would change? She couldn't stop it. Normal change was one thing and not particularly welcome at that.

Walking into a situation that held as much threat as promise was quite another.

His voice grew husky. "Don't you ever want more for yourself than to run your father's home?"

Did she? She allowed a door to creak open so she could see inside where her secret longings and denied dreams resided. What she saw filled her with an ache as wide as the Dakota horizon. She longed for more. She wanted it all—her own home, a husband who loved her, children added to Dorrie's sweet presence. It was impossible. Unattainable.

Frighteningly different.

She closed her eyes and prayed for wisdom and common sense.

Colby's whisper persisted. "Don't you wish you could have your own home? Your own family?"

Eyes still closed, she nodded slowly.

"Then trust me."

Her eyes flashed wide as she realized what stood in the way of doing so. "I need to know what makes you run." Giving him the benefit of doubt, she corrected herself. "Made you run." Until she did, it would be a specter hovering in the corners, able to send him down the road if the conditions gave it more strength.

She rose with as much dignity as her shaking limbs allowed and head held high by dint of her rigid self-control, she returned home.

That should have been the end of it. But how could it be when he joined them for every meal, when she had but to look out the window to glimpse him at work and when her heart continued to ache after him. When he spoke words of encouragement to her and offered so much leadership to Alex.

She couldn't seem to turn around without memories of him.

He'd sat in that chair holding a skein of yarn for Rose and listening to Anna's spelling words.

He'd stood at her side at the cupboard washing

dishes as she dried, telling her of the stampede of cattle in a vicious storm when he was but fourteen and on his first cattle drive.

He'd stood in the middle of the front room and stared in awe as she came from her room in her new outfit, one Rose had made 'specially for the Christmas program.

Even the church was full of memories—current ones of singing and playing music together, sharing bits and pieces of the years they'd been apart—intermingled with the past when he had eagerly listened to every word Father spoke as if seeking something to fill a vast hunger.

Why did he run? If she understood perhaps she could trust him not to do so again.

But until then…

Chapter Eleven

Colby stepped into the kitchen as familiar as any home he'd ever known. The aroma of fried chops, apples and cinnamon greeted him. He closed his eyes and inhaled the scents and felt a sensation of peace and blessing. This is what home should be like, not the fear-filled uncertainty of his younger years. "Smells great in here."

"Anna made apple pandowdy," Alex said. "She makes the best in the world."

"Alex," Anna scolded. "How would you know?" She smiled apologetically at Colby.

As their gazes connected he acknowledged that all he'd wanted all his life was right here in this room, in the smile of one woman—Anna. Why he'd left her even once was beyond understanding. Yet he had done so twice, three times if he counted Nora. But now he wanted to be with her, together with Dorrie, part of Anna's life forever. He was trying to trust God to make it possible yet the one thing she wanted he could not give—the reason he had left. He could have said because he feared he would become like his pa. She would have understood that. But it wasn't honesty and he wanted nothing but the truth between them.

What about what you did?

He could never tell her that awful truth. It was part of what he had left behind. Pastor Caldwell assured him that God forgave and forgot the past. Colby intended to do the same.

Yet what if his past found him? It scared him through and through. He hoped no one noticed how stiff his joints seemed as he moved to the table and sank to a chair.

Over the meal, the Caldwells frequently shared how his or her day had gone. He remembered this ritual from when he was younger, remembered how foreign it had seemed at first. He couldn't have imagined sharing around the table with his pa. He learned to keep his mouth shut and his eyes open, ready to duck if necessary.

But the practice had made something deep inside him feel warm and welcome.

It still did.

After initial awkwardness with him sitting at the table, they had resumed the habit.

Alex barely waited for his father to say "Amen" before he bounced to the edge of his chair. "The race is coming up. I'm going to try and win the hundred-yard dash."

Colby kept his opinion to himself. He'd only once or twice seen the boy move faster than a snail's pace. But his enthusiasm was commendable. "I could help you practice." He'd gone to school so seldom but one teacher, Mr. Gates, had taken an interest in making sure Colby could both read and run. Colby grinned. Two skills he found equally useful throughout his life.

"Would you? Great."

Alex's gratitude made him grin. He glanced at Anna and saw her gleaming smile. She mouthed the words *thank you.* His heart swelled up his throat, making it impossible to swallow until he jerked his gaze away. She'd been truly friendly since the day they had talked about the men coming to the church. Friendly but reserved. Waiting for the answer he couldn't give. Anna told how Dorrie had said please so clearly. But her eyes shared so much more with Colby—mutual love of this child, and if he looked deep…hope for more. She turned to her father.

"How was your day, Father?"

Anna's question slid through his mind like fresh cream, sweet and smooth. He understood it wasn't what she said but the sound of her voice that had this effect on him. Slowly he lifted his head to steal a glance at her as she spoke to her father. If only he knew the answer as to why he ran, he would willingly give it. But he'd told her all he knew— he believed he had nothing to offer her.

He remembered the power of prayer. *Father God, help me understand what made me feel I had to leave.*

"The Booker family are all feeling better. I enjoyed a pleasant afternoon in their company."

Colby stared at the pastor, wondering at the way he ducked his head. Totally unlike the directness he expected but no one else seemed to notice and Colby decided he had a suspicious nature.

Three pairs of eyes turned toward Colby. It was his turn. "I finished fixing the roof today."

"Good," Pastor Caldwell said.

Colby checked for Anna's reaction, expecting a smile of happiness at his progress. Instead, her eyes turned dark and bottomless. She held his gaze and in that moment he was sure he felt a promise and a wish.

Then Alex passed her the potatoes and she looked away.

Had she thought how he would soon be finished? Did she wonder if he would leave? Wanting to put her mind at rest he spoke again. "I see Rawlings is looking for help at the feed mill. How long has he had that sign up?"

"Seems it's always up. Hear he's a hard man to work for, though perhaps only because he expects an honest day's work for an honest day's pay."

Colby kept his attention on the pastor as he spoke. "I could promise that." He stole a glance at Anna and in that unguarded moment, her eyes flared, revealing the depth of her feeling for him. He turned his attention to the meal as joy filled his heart with rich strains of music.

"One of the best meals I've ever eaten," he said a little while later.

"Thank you." She pushed back. "Alex, clear up the table while I put soup bones to cook." She reached for Dorrie.

"I'll get her," he offered.

She nodded and smiled as she hurried to the stove.

He lifted his daughter and stole a moment's hug.

Dorrie patted his chin. "Owie," she said as she felt his whiskers.

He laughed and waggled his chin. "Scratchy, aren't they?"

She giggled then squirmed to be down. He lowered her to the floor but kept hold of her as he reached for the cloth on the cupboard and dipped it in the basin of water. "Let's wash supper off your face."

Dorrie lifted her face to him and let him wipe it clean.

He bent and kissed her plump cheeks then released her with a pat on the bottom. "There you go, little miss."

She pushed a chair to the cupboard. "Me help."

Anna rubbed the back of her hand over her brow. "Sweetie, Mama's got to peel this onion." She shot a glance at Colby. "I want to simmer the bones overnight."

"Me help."

Colby chuckled. "Let's do dishes together." He shifted Dorrie's chair to the cupboard and let her put her hands in the soapy water. As Alex brought him the dishes, Colby leaned over Dorrie, reaching around her to wash.

He would never get tired of the smell of his child, the way her hair tickled his chin as he helped her wash the dishes. He wished the moment could last forever but all too soon the dishes were done.

Wanting—needing—to share his joy in this child, he turned to Anna, hoping to see her eyes soften with understanding. Instead, her eyes narrowed with warning. And though she never spoke a word, he heard her clearly.

Don't think of taking her away. I won't let you.

His joy plunged to the pit of his stomach. He had

ruined so many things. Was it possible he could undo any of it?

With God's help perhaps. Time alone would tell if God chose to give him such an undeserved blessing. In the meantime, he wasn't leaving. How long would it take Anna to accept that as fact?

"Did you mean it when you said you'd help me practice for the race?" Alex asked.

"Of course. Tomorrow after school if it's all right with Anna."

"As soon as your chores are done. But you aren't to interfere with Colby's work."

"I won't." He hurried to tackle his homework.

"Thank you, Colby." Anna's voice was sharp with warning but softened with gratitude.

"I've done nothing."

"You've offered to help Alex. That's something."

He held on to hope. Perhaps she would begin to see just how they needed each other.

Colby had looked in vain for some sign of Hugh. The man must have been angry when Colby left after accusing him of such dreadful things. Colby knew he had not done anything shifty with Nora. The man had done nothing but help. Maybe Hugh was still mad enough to stay away. He hoped not. Hugh had been the one person besides Anna and her family who saw him as more than a drunken bum. He really wanted to find him and tell him he was sorry for his stupid words.

He asked the men who had gathered in the church again to hear more about God if they knew where he could find Hugh.

"Hugh's gone," Tobias said, his voice slow with sadness.

"Gone?" Shock numbed his cheeks. "Dead?"

"Nah. Gone to the Black Hills looking for gold."

Colby's breath whooshed out. "Scared me for a minute."

Arty let out an expansive sigh. "Could be dead by now. I hear the camps are pretty rough places."

Slink waved an unsteady hand. "Hugh knows how to take care of himself."

"No one's heard from him?" Colby asked.

"No one's said so."

"I wonder how a person could locate him?" Now it seemed he must find Hugh. Make sure he was alive.

Tobias rubbed his whiskery chin making a raspy sound. "Suppose you could write to the sheriff in one of the towns and ask after him."

"Good idea. Maybe I'll do that. Thanks for your help."

If he could locate Hugh and make things right between them, it would be one less thing from his past to haunt him.

But one thing would forever haunt him.

He waved goodbye to the men before he allowed the worst thing from his past to fill his mind.

There was no way he could undo it. The best he could hope for was to hide from it.

"So we all know what we are to do for the party?" Mrs. Percy checked around the circle. The ladies' sewing group had assembled again in the front room of the manse to plan the lunch the church would serve at the town birthday party. The usual people attended. It was nice to see Mrs. Booker, wan but able to be up and about. She had brought her sister, Grace Weaver, who wore a pretty gray dress. Anna decided Miss Weaver was almost as pretty as Rose had been.

The ladies murmured agreement to Mrs. Percy's question. They had gone over the arrangements a number of times. Anna was certain everyone had memorized the details by now but Mrs. Percy was a stickler for wanting things perfect.

"Now about the booth downtown."

There followed a flurry of suggestions.

Anna tried to concentrate on the business at hand as each one listed the items they would donate to sell at the booth to help fund a library for the town, but her thoughts insisted on drifting over to the church where Colby worked.

With each passing day she found it increasingly hard to keep Colby from invading her mind. Every moment they were apart she ached to be with him. Yet when she was with him, her caution made it impossible to fully enjoy his presence.

She was turning into a fussy old woman.

Mrs. Percy cleared her throat, alerting Anna to pay attention as an important item was to be introduced.

"Mr. Percy says the repairs are coming along well."

Anna nodded, pleased for the faint praise on Colby's behalf.

"I'm concerned, however—"

Anna sat up straight. Mrs. Percy's "howevers" usually meant "oh, no" for Anna.

"Are you all aware of what's going on at the church many evenings?"

Anna's heart bolted for her mouth. Had people seen her going over to spend time with Colby? Had they deemed it inappropriate? Even though it had been perfectly innocent, necessary practice for the Sunday hymns, she should have been more careful.

"Unsavory characters hanging about." She fixed Anna with a stern look. "Are you aware of this?"

Oh, only the men visiting Colby.

It took a full minute for Anna's heart to resume its normal pace. "Of course. Father says the church welcomes sinners."

Mrs. Klein nodded. "That's a fact."

"I just think it's suspicious. Colby Bloxham and his old friends." The word was accompanied with a sniff. "Could be they're drinking."

Anna stilled her features not to smile at the woman's distress over such an idea. Then her amusement faded. She'd been equally suspicious and it was every bit as ludicrous on her behalf. "They've come to learn about God."

Mrs. Percy's mouth flopped open. She seemed to struggle with the idea. "Well." *Huff.*

"Why, isn't that wonderful." It was Miss Weaver. "Exactly the sort of people our Lord would have sought out when He was on earth."

Mrs. Percy's eyebrows headed for her hairline. "Exactly the sort He would have driven from the temple, I say. 'My house is the house of prayer, but ye have made it a den of thieves.'"

Miss Weaver smiled gently. "I must have misunderstood. I thought young Colby has repented and asked for salvation."

Anna watched in awe. She had never seen anyone stand up to Mrs. Percy but despite how Miss Weaver spoke calmly, it was a duel as brisk as any with swords.

Mrs. Klein dared to enter the foray. "I understood the same thing."

"Well, praise God." Miss Weaver said with a gentle smile. "He is no longer the Colby you remember, is he? God's word says 'If any man be in Christ he is a new creature, old things are passed away; behold, all things are become new.'"

Anna's respect for Mrs. Booker's sister grew. Yet the words troubled her. She believed God's word. Heaven forbid otherwise. But was Colby a new creature? Was he changed or was this life convenient for now? After all, hadn't he acted much the same before Rose died? Was this any more real?

Mrs. Percy smiled, a look as full of challenge as anything. "In Galatians, Chapter 6, and also First Corinthians, Chapter 4, Verse 2, if I don't miss my mark—"

Anna knew—as did everyone else—that Mrs. Percy seldom missed her mark.

"We are warned that a man must prove himself."

Exactly. That's what Anna wanted—Colby to prove himself before she could trust her heart to him again.

Miss Weaver nodded. "I perceive you are a true student of the word."

Heads jerked from Mrs. Percy to Miss Weaver, and Anna guessed the rest of the ladies were as keen to see how this exchange would end as she.

"But to whom must he prove himself? Does not the word warn us in Romans, Chapter 14, Verse 4, if I remember correctly but then I fear I am not the expert student you are, that 'to his own master he standeth or falleth.' Is it not the Lord's work to change him? As it says in Philippians, Chapter 2, Verse 13, 'It is God which worketh in you both to will and to do of His good pleasure.' Perhaps we need to trust God to do His work."

A couple of the women nodded. Mrs. Percy knew to say anything more would make her seem unchristian but Anna understood she wasn't convinced.

Neither was Anna. Not that she didn't trust that God could change people, but she wasn't about to risk everything until she saw undeniable evidence Colby had changed. After all, he couldn't even say what made him leave, so how could he be certain it wouldn't happen again? And if he left once more, would he take more than her heart if she gave it to him?

Would he take Dorrie?

She had to clench her hands together to still the pain accompanying the thought.

Mrs. Percy found another bone to gnaw. "What about the cross? I assume a new one will be ready in time for the celebration."

Anna pulled her thoughts back to the demands

of the moment and nodded. "Father is taking care of it." When she asked, Father assured her he and Colby had it in hand. She was not privy to their conversations, so had no idea exactly what was being done. But she trusted that if Father said it would be done, it would.

Chapter Twelve

Supper was over and the pastor had gone to the front room. That left Colby alone in the kitchen with Anna. Now was his chance. He would take care of this business of composing a letter to Hugh. "I want to write to a friend and wondered if I could get a piece of paper from you."

"Of course." She slipped into the front room and returned with a sheet of paper and a pencil. "You're welcome to sit at the table to write."

He accepted her offer and licked the end of the pencil then bent over the page. As always the words refused to form in his mind so he could put them to paper. He should start with "dear sheriff" but was it *der?* No that wasn't right. *Deer, dere?* He sighed. The only thing he knew for certain was it started with *D*. He bent over the paper and laboriously made the first letter. He paused, leaned back, tried to remember how to spell the word. Nothing came. How would he manage *sheriff* when he couldn't spell *dear?*

The pencil snapped between his fingers. Guilt at destroying the precious instrument crashed with frustration. "I'm sorry," he muttered at Anna's surprised glance, meaning the broken pencil.

"It's not a problem."

He bent his head, wishing she would look elsewhere. He didn't want her to see his inability to write a simple letter. He read passably well, had managed to hide the fact from both Rose and Anna that he had trouble writing. How would she react?

His old man had jeered and called him stupid.

Only now did he realize the hurtful words came from a man who signed his name with an *X*.

Somehow the knowing should have made him feel better about being able to do more.

But it didn't.

Anna moved closer.

He felt her stop at his side. Knew she studied the page. She'd have to be blind to not see the crudely made letter and stupid not to realize his difficulty. She was neither.

"Do you need some help?" Her quiet voice seemed to carry no opinion.

"I don't write very good." His throat clenched

around the words allowing each to escape as a tight croak.

"I can write for you…unless you don't want me to know what your letter says."

His relief was so palpable he wondered it didn't plop to the table quivering like warm pudding. "Nothing private about it at all." He shoved the paper and sharpened bit of pencil toward her.

She pulled out a chair and sat at his elbow. So close he could smell bits of cinnamon and basil, and the clean fragrance of her soap.

He shifted, rested his arm on the back of her chair, barely an inch from touching her.

She bent over the paper, exposing the pearly white of her slender neck. "You dictate and I'll write."

He struggled to remember what he wanted to say. Her nearness made it impossible to think. He loved her. Plain and simple. He continued to pray she would give him another chance to prove himself worthy of her love.

She turned toward him. "Colby, what did you want me to write?"

Her eyes filled with golden color that came from streaks of light brown alternating with darker brown. Her lips parted in surprise at the way he stared at her and she looked expectant as if she wanted more from him. Like a kiss? How he ached to kiss her, but he dare not until he knew she would welcome him with a heart of trust.

It took every scrap of his mental strength to pull his gaze from hers and stare at the page.

She jerked her attention the same direction.

He removed his arm from the chair back and planted his hands firmly on his knee. "I'm trying to find a friend." He could barely grate the words out. "But I don't know where he is." The tightness in his throat relaxed as he thought about Hugh. "I'm going to write a sheriff on the off chance that might locate him."

She nodded, her head bent over the paper.

"Dear Sheriff," he began. "My name is Colby Bloxham. You might have heard of me in the past. I am no longer that man. I am now a good, God-fearing man." He paused. "Just put 'a God-fearing man.'" He didn't know if anyone would call him good. Not yet. He waited until she erased the word then continued dictating. "I'm looking for my friend Hugh Mackenzie. Is there any chance you have heard of him? If so, could you let him know Colby wants to hear from him? He can contact me at Steveville, Dakota Territory." He spoke slowly as Anna wrote the words, amazed at how quickly the beautiful script appeared at her hands.

"That's about it I guess."

She put the pencil down and leaned back. Her shoulder brushed his.

He steeled himself to keep from wrapping his arms around her and pressing her to his chest where she would surely feel the demanding beat of his heart.

She pushed back. "I'll get an envelope."

It took concentrated effort to force air into his lungs. He held it there waiting for sanity and reality to replace the trembling of his thoughts.

She returned and stood across the table from him. "How shall I address it?"

He'd thought it through and decided on the most likely place. "The Sheriff, Lead, Dakota Territory. He went looking for gold."

She wrote the words on the envelope then handed it to him.

He folded the letter neatly, tucked it inside and sealed the flap. "Thank you. I'll mail it tomorrow."

She smiled, something warm and understanding in her gaze. "Glad to help and I hope you find your friend." She ducked her head and when she looked at him again he saw uncertainty in her eyes.

His blood felt thick as it pushed through his veins. He did not want to hear again how she couldn't get over him leaving in the past, so he headed for the door. He paused only long enough to thank her again then chased his regrets outside.

* * *

Anna stared after him, her mind in a whirl. Since the ladies had left, Miss Weaver's words had haunted her. Was God changing him? Could she trust God? Yes. But Colby...

Not, she knew, without evidence.

And how she longed to see that evidence and be able to recapture the sweet bonds they had once shared.

Lord, help us regain the trust and closeness we once had. Now, if it be Your will, please show me if it's safe to trust him.

The next day was busier than usual. Dorrie got into a hundred things before the day was an hour old and from there she gained steam.

In her haste to catch up, Anna sloshed the dishwater and ended up washing the floor unexpectedly.

Little annoyances built one on another.

She paused as a bout of tears threatened. Why was she letting things bother her?

She knew the answer. Because she cared for Colby. He'd laid claim to a great portion of her heart. She'd only been sixteen when he left and yet he continually filled her hopes and dreams for the future. How she ached for the closeness of the past.

How foolish her thoughts...to want the very thing that could destroy her. With great effort she pushed stubborn resolve into her heart. She could not allow him to hurt her again.

The day sped past. Alex came home from school and slipped out to do his chores.

Out the window, she watched Alex and Colby talking. Alex leaned over as if waiting for a signal to run. Colby leaned over, too, planting splayed fingers on the ground. He must be showing Alex how to start a race.

She smiled and tucked away this little picture of just what a good man Colby was.

As she watched, she mixed up cake batter. She turned to put more coal in the stove to keep the oven at an even temperature. The coal bucket was empty. One of Alex's chores was to fill it. Anna sighed. He might want to run but when it came to chores he was slower than a spring thaw. She grabbed the bucket and headed to the shed.

Colby was right about one thing. She coddled Alex. He needed to grow up and accept the few responsibilities he had. She must speak to him.

Colby and Alex came in for supper a little later, both of them grinning with eagerness.

"Colby says I'm a good runner."

"You've got potential. A little practice and perseverance and you'll do fine." The smile Colby sent Anna's direction melted away a great deal of the day's tension. It was good to have him here. His presence seemed to give each moment a slice of calmness. She wished he could stay longer, share a few more hours but he spent his nights elsewhere. And tonight when she relished every minute, he left early, saying he expected Slink and a few others to stop by.

As soon as he left, she forced herself to deal with Alex. "What about your chores after school?"

A guilty look flitted across his face. "Forgot," he mumbled.

"I shouldn't have to remind you all the time. You're old enough to be responsible. For the next two days, you're confined to your bedroom after school."

"That's not fair," he yelled. "It's just a bucket of coal."

Dorrie's eyes grew big. She looked from Anna to Alex, her little mouth round with concern. Anna patted her hand, silently assuring her.

"It's your job. I have enough to do."

"It's sissy work. I'm too old for it. Besides, Colby is training me to run."

"You can train again after you've spent some time in your room. Hopefully it will help you remember your responsibilities in the future."

He pushed back so hard his chair fell with a clatter. "Stop treating me like a baby." He rushed to his room.

Dorrie whimpered.

"It's okay, sweetie." But it wasn't. Her whole life frayed apart before her eyes. She wanted it back, neat and orderly. She didn't want things to change, especially this way.

Alex should have helped with dishes but she didn't want to deal with his anger, so she did them alone, even though she realized it probably defeated the purpose of confining him to his room in the hopes he'd learn responsibility.

By the time she got Dorrie in bed, Anna wanted nothing more than to lie down and cry. Knowing that served no purpose, she did what she learned to do throughout previous times of trial. She headed to the church to pray, pausing at the door to make sure Colby's friends had departed. Hearing no sound, she crept in through the front door. Colby sat in a pew near the front, his head bent as if reading.

She didn't want to attract his attention, needed to think about him without his presence invading her thoughts so she tiptoed into the cloakroom. She needed to sit in front of the cross and find peace. She stopped in the middle of the tiny room and blinked.

The cross was gone.

The frustrations of the day boiled over, filling her with despair-laced anger. She spun around and stomped into the sanctuary.

Colby, hearing her, turned to face her.

"It's gone. One of your friends must have taken it."

"What are you talking about?"

"The cross. Where is it?" The enormity of her loss sucked the strength from her knees and she sank to the nearest pew. Her anger melted into sorrow. A sob caught in her throat where she trapped it. Her reaction left her feeling foolish and vulnerable.

"It's safe."

"Where is it? Who's taken it?"

"Trust me."

The words mocked her, drove spikes through her thoughts. Trust? The one thing she wanted to do but seemed unable to. She'd even prayed for a chance to test it. Was this an opportunity?

Memories assailed her. She could barely remember her mother except for a fleeting picture of her in a beautiful steel-blue dress and a feathered hat, bending over Anna to kiss her cheek. The whiff of flower-scented toilet water.

But she could never forget the wagon flipping over, the incredible agony of learning to live without Rose, of having to clean out Timmy's belongings. The sob she'd held back escaped in a gentle wail. "It hurts so much to lose the people you love. I think it would be easier to never care about people."

Praying at the cross had held her together through it all. She sucked in air, forcing back sobs she feared would tear her apart if she let them out. "I want the cross back."

"You'll get it. Trust me." His words sounded like a promise. He sat beside her and tucked his arm around her shoulders, pulling her close. "Not everyone leaves. And whatever you face, God will never leave you."

She searched his eyes, found an undeniable strength there. She let his promise, his strength reach deep into her being and filter into the dusty chambers she'd kept locked for years. The doors cracked open and she discovered that his smile had cleansed the room. He reminded her of where she got her strength—God, and he offered what she wanted and needed—his promise, his presence. She had only to take one small step into her fears to get it all.

His eyes filled with soft evening light. "I won't disappoint you."

She considered all he asked, measured it against what she had to lose. If it was only the cross, she could bear it. It was only a symbol of God's love and grace, which flowed freely without need of a damaged piece of wood.

But her heart…that was something else entirely.

She couldn't risk breaking it again. Doubted she would survive another time of loving and losing.

Firmly she shoved the doors to the secret, dark places closed.

"I'm sure whatever you and Father decide will suit." She returned to the house, her insides more knotted than when she left, not from external stresses but from her inner turmoil.

Colby's chest muscles didn't release their vice-like tension until Anna slipped out the door and crossed the yard, her steps firm, her shoulders back, her spine rigid. Not until she entered the house did his thoughts spring into action.

She would trust her father, but refused to trust him. Not that he could blame her but his whole heart and soul longed for her love and trust.

Would she ever give it?

Would he ever be worthy of it?

He collapsed on the pew and buried his head in his hands. How could he prove he was different? *Lord God, show me a way.*

A few minutes later he left the church. With God's help he would not disappoint her again.

The next week was extremely busy with the day of the big celebration approaching. He pushed to get the final touches done to the repairs and enlisted the help of several of his friends. He also involved them with his plans for the cross.

A group of people descended on the church two days before the big event. In the cemetery, the men cut grass, pruned scraggly trees and scoured the tombstones. Inside, the women washed windows, scrubbed the floor and polished pews.

Colby cleaned up the materials and equipment from his work. As he stood back to admire the result, several people gathered at his side.

"Good as new." It was an elderly gent who had come inside to borrow a broom.

Mrs. Percy stood at the front of the sanctuary staring at the wall behind the pulpit, which had been returned from the room above the saloon. "Where's the cross? Shouldn't it be in place? Who is in charge of that detail?"

Pastor Caldwell stepped to the woman's side. "I am."

"Well, where is it?"

"We'll have it in place on the seventeenth." Despite the woman's fussing, the pastor refused to say anything more.

Colby met Anna's gaze across the room as she polished the piano. He felt in her look the same questions and doubts Mrs. Percy expressed.

Trust me. You'll see.

Asking her to trust him about the cross would give him a chance to prove himself. If she would only take this one little step perhaps she would see that more was possible.

They looked long and hard at each other until she finally jerked away, her attention claimed by someone wanting to know where to put a lamp.

Colby let out a frustrated sigh. Her expression had not shifted one bit. Would nothing ever change?

The work bee ended. The church was ready.

The next day another crowd descended and long plank tables soon filled the yard. Colby glimpsed Anna hurrying from one task to another.

Determined to speak to her, to urge her to trust him about the cross, he edged around the crowd, planning to catch her as she trotted toward the house for yet another errand.

He fell in beside her.

"Can I help?"

"All the seats need to be wiped off. Can you do that?"

"Of course. I'm willing to do whatever I can to ease your responsibilities." He meant so much more than preparing for the birthday celebration.

He wanted to share her life.

"Anna, we had so much. Can't—"

She handed him a basin and a rag. "There's hot water in the reservoir."

He wanted to talk. But now was not the time and

he filled the basin with water and wiped the benches.

After a community-style lunch with everyone contributing, Colby headed to the little shack where Tobias lived and where they'd been working on the cross.

Every street in town looked as if it had been swept. Every window gleamed. The storefronts had either been repainted or scrubbed, all in preparation for the upcoming birthday celebration. Colby felt pride at the way the town showed its solidarity, and excitement at the little part he'd had in the upcoming party.

Slink, Tobias and eight others crowded the tiny room when Colby arrived.

"It's almost finished," Slink said.

Colby admired the handwork. "It's beautiful." He hoped Anna would see the love that had gone into every detail.

Chapter Thirteen

June 17

The day the town had prepared and planned for the past six months.

Anna checked Dorrie. She looked perfect in her white dress and stockings. And it didn't matter in the least that she would come home at the end of the day dusty and soiled.

She stepped to the street, turned as she heard the church door click. Colby paused on the step.

Thankfully, the past few days had been busy, leaving them little opportunity to talk and even less to be alone, which suited her just fine. She wasn't sure how to deal with the longing to trust him, the feeling that somehow trusting God and trusting Colby were linked.

Because they felt so totally different. She had no trouble trusting God. He loved her. But trusting Colby was another matter entirely. She'd once thought he loved her. As she loved him. But she had misjudged his feelings.

Trusting him again would take time. And proof.

Dorrie saw him. "Da-da," she chirped, and Colby moved to take Dorrie's hand.

Anna's heartbeat picked up pace as she saw he meant to accompany them. Despite her misgivings, she could not pretend her love for him had died. Although she'd done her best to quench it.

They headed toward the heart of town.

The main street had been closed off and turned into a fairground. Booths lined each side of the street—one selling popcorn, another with a fishing game, yet another with a guess-your-weight challenge, and past that, a test-your-strength bell.

Alex came by with a couple of schoolmates as Colby and Anna stood in front of the strength game. "Try it out, Colby."

"We'll both do it." He paid a penny for each of them as a crowd gathered round cheering him on. He wiped his hands then grabbed the hammer and swung it over his head and hit the pad at the bottom. The metal indicator shot upward, stopped three quarters of the way up and dropped down.

The spectators jeered and laughed.

He handed the mallet to Alex.

Alex hesitated. "I can't do that good."

"No one expects you to, but you might be surprised at how well you do." Colby squeezed Alex's upper arm. "Feels to me like you've put on an inch or two here."

"You think so?"

"Give it a try."

Alex widened his stance and swung with all his might, groaning when the indicator went about halfway.

Colby clapped him on the back. "Let's see if your friends can beat that." He paid a penny for each of the boys gathered round. And when only one, a big lad, beat Alex, he grinned as widely as if Alex had handed him a trophy. "What did I tell you? Nothing like hard work to build muscles."

Alex puffed out his chest.

Anna hid a grin. It was nice to see Alex growing up. She sobered instantly. What had Laura said? He'd grow up and leave home. Anna wanted to pull him back and protect him from all that growing up meant.

But her sudden fear couldn't survive amidst all the fun of the day.

Colby grinned at the men crowded round him. "Who can ring the bell?"

Mike, a big farm boy, paid his penny and tried. He beat Colby by one mark.

Colby clapped. "Come on. Who's next?"

Men pushed closer, vying for a turn to pay for the chance to outdo each other.

Colby leaned over and whispered in Anna's ear, "This will end up making a lot of money."

The funds raised throughout the day were to go to providing a library.

Anna laughed as she understood he egged the others on until the bottle beside the machine reached almost to the top and Father came along and emptied it.

Colby certainly would benefit the fundraiser. The town could use a man like this changed Colby.

Watching him laugh and enjoy the crowd filled her heart with admiration, made the whole scene dance with color and enjoyment. She teetered on the edge of giving up her resistance to him.

But as Dorrie tugged at her hand, she was jerked back to reality. Colby could leave as quickly and easily as he returned. What was to stop him? Neither she nor Dorrie had been enough in the past.

What drove him away?

Responsibilities? Her? She must know before she released the locks on her heart.

Dorrie grabbed her father's hand. "Go," she said.

Colby and Anna exchanged glances and laughed. Their gazes clung. Anna's cheeks grew warm at the look in his eyes. And then Dorrie jerked at them.

She blinked back her feelings. How easily she forgot to be cautious.

They moved on to a puppet show. Dorrie screamed with laughter when the puppets tripped over each other and flew through the air.

They moved on to the bake and craft sale being held under shelter of the hotel portico. Anna picked up a pretty pinafore.

"Did you make this, Miss Weaver?"

Miss Weaver chuckled, a merry sound. "Please call me Grace. And, yes, I made that little thing. I seem to have more time on my hands than I know what to do with."

"It's beautiful." It would fit Dorrie and although she needed a new one, Anna could make one for far less. She went to put it down but Colby plucked it from her fingers and held it in front of Dorrie.

"It's the right size, isn't it?"

"Yes, but—"

"I'll take it." He paid Grace.

They walked on. "I planned to make her a new one," Anna whispered. "It wouldn't cost near that much."

"I thought I'd save you the effort. Seems to me you work hard enough as it is."

No one ever worried that she might have too much work to do. No one even offered to help. Knowing Colby noticed made Anna almost stumble on the wooden sidewalk, not because it was rough but because of her surprise.

She pinched her nose to stop the sting of tears.

Thankfully the mayor spared her from embarrassing herself. Using a bullhorn, he announced games and races over at the schoolyard. Much of the crowd drifted that direction.

If only she could give her heart fully to Colby she could enjoy his support and encouragement every day. For a moment, the idea almost capsized her stubbornness. But again, her doubts prevailed.

A race for toddlers was announced first.

Colby squatted in front of Dorrie. "Do you want to run?"

She nodded. "I run." She took off instantly.

Colby grabbed her. "Wait a minute. We'll go to the start line."

Anna laughed as he tried to explain the event to Dorrie who babbled and squirmed, trying to escape.

"I run, Da-da." Her feet churned as Colby lifted her off the ground and carried her to the marked spot.

Anna giggled at mothers and fathers trying to sort out children under the age of three and explain the concept of a race.

"Go to the finish line," Colby said. "I'll head her in your direction."

Anna did as he suggested and soon one parent of each child did the same.

Someone hollered go and the children were released.

"Dorrie, come to Mama," Anna called. A dozen other parents yelled at their offspring. She wondered how anyone could make out who called whom. The names were indiscernible in the melee.

Dorrie veered toward a little boy with a ball in his hands.

"Dorrie, no. This way."

Dorrie ignored her and tackled the boy. They tumbled to the ground, the boy shrieking for his mother.

Anna shook her head. She found Colby's face in the crowd and laughed at his stunned look.

Then they joined the race to separate the two. Colby got there first and scooped Dorrie off her victim. She clutched the ball triumphantly.

"Ball. Mine."

"'Fraid not, honey. Give it back."

Dorrie held on with all her might. "Mine."

Anna stood a few inches away but didn't intervene. She couldn't wait to see how Colby would deal with this stubborn side of his sweet little daughter.

Meanwhile the little boy continued to scream as his parents tried to console him.

"You have to give it back," Colby insisted. "It belongs to that little boy."

"No." Dorrie stuck out her chin.

Anna knew the look and settled back on her heels. Colby had two choices—wrestle the ball from Dorrie's hands, or divert her so she let it go.

Colby looked at her, silently pleading for help. Grinning, she shrugged. *She's your daughter. You deal with her.*

He apparently got her silent message for he sighed and rolled his eyes, which sent Anna into a fit of giggles.

"Dorrie, my dear sweet child, if you give back the ball I'll buy you a candy stick."

Dorrie looked at the ball, looked at her father as if to measure his sincerity.

"Ball." She handed it to the sobbing boy. "Canny," she said to Colby.

Colby grinned triumphantly as they joined Anna.

"Bribery," she murmured. "I can't believe you'd stoop to bribery."

"I was about ready to do anything to end that scene." He grinned at Anna and they both laughed.

And without her permission her heart claimed the day for its own to enjoy. Even if he left again, she would at least have this one day to cherish.

They found a candy booth and Colby purchased

a red-and-white barber-striped candy then they returned to the games in time to hear a race for twelve- to fourteen-year-old boys announced.

Alex headed toward the start line then stopped, uncertainty apparent in his expression.

Colby handed Dorrie to Anna and hurried to Alex's side.

She followed, curious about what he intended.

He leaned close to Alex.

Anna strained to hear his soft words. "This is great practice. You can see how all the things I taught you work in a real race. Never mind if you win or lose. Concentrate on your technique."

Alex nodded and strode to the start, his head high.

Anna shot Colby a look of thanks but his gaze remained on Alex. He mouthed words. She realized he repeated instructions he must have taught Alex.

"That's it. Get into a good position."

Ready. Set. Go. They were off. When Alex gained the lead from the first step, Anna cheered so loud Dorrie jumped. "Look, sweetie. Alex is running. He might win."

Dorrie yelled loudly though she likely had no idea why.

Colby shot a glance at his noisy daughter, his gaze brushed Anna and they laughed as if the moment held wonderful significance.

She hoped it did.

Alex led the pack. A bigger lad gained but Alex crossed the finish line first. His grin at winning rivaled the sunshine for brightness.

Alex had always been shy about competing, didn't like to do anything where he might fail. Anna had never known such pride in her brother marred only by the certainty that this was another step away from her.

"Now for all the men."

Colby acted like he didn't hear.

Anna nudged him. "This is your race."

"Nah, I don't think so."

"Of course you'll run."

Alex reached his side. "Come on, Colby. Show them how it's done."

Colby scrubbed the back of his hand over his chin. "I don't know. Don't you think I'm too grown up for this?"

Alex grabbed his hand and dragged him away.

Colby chuckled as they trotted over to the start.

Anna moved down the side where she had an unobstructed view. Colby flashed her a grin that shot through all her defenses and landed somewhere south of her heart. She loved him. Despite uncertainty about the future, despite everything, she loved him.

Today she would simply accept the fact.

Tomorrow she would deal with reality.

She cheered as the race began. He slowed as he drew even with her to flash her another grin and it cost him the race. Not that he seemed to mind. He was in high spirits as he rejoined her.

They watched the horse races. They shared a huge bag of popcorn. Anna realized she would have enjoyed anything in Colby's company, knowing she loved him, all doubts and fears silenced for the day.

Later they bought sandwiches and pie at the food booth, then it was time to go home and prepare for the evening activities.

Anna's face stung from too long in the sun. And Dorrie's cheeks were far too red even though Anna had tried to keep a bonnet on her. She sponged their faces carefully and put on a clean dress. She put the new pinafore over Dorrie's dress and smoothed her hair.

In the other rooms she could hear Father and Alex preparing.

She smiled at Dorrie. "We're ready."

Dorrie nodded. "I wedy."

They hurried to the church. Already the sanctuary was crowded. More people gathered outside. Anna made her way to the front and handed Dorrie to Laura.

She began to play the hymns, her throat tightening when Colby joined in, playing the mouth organ as he stood to the side of the piano. Their gazes connected and she smiled. Something wrenched inside her, a combination of sweetness and fear. She'd always protected her heart. Life had taught the value of doing so. But her love for Colby could not be denied. For whatever time she had, she would enjoy it and pray she would survive if he left.

The music drifted around her and through her. This was one thing they shared without reservation. She let him take the melody and improvised an accompaniment. A hush fell over the crowd. She knew the congregation enjoyed the music as much as she and Colby.

Father went to the pulpit. He welcomed everyone then announced the first hymn.

Anna could enjoy sharing music with Colby for a few more minutes.

She'd prepared a solo, practicing with Colby accompanying her on the mouth organ and went to the pulpit when Father nodded to her. The hymn she'd chosen was an old Charles Wesley one, "O for a thousand tongues to sing my great Redeemer's praise."

It fit perfectly with her feelings and for this occasion of meeting in the church again.

She finished and sat beside Laura, her heart so

full of joy and love it forced tears to her eyes. She blinked them away.

Colby slid in beside her.

She daren't look at him even when Dorrie scrambled from Laura's knee across Anna and straight to her father's lap.

Anna felt Laura watching her and composed her face before glancing at her and giving a quick shrug as if to say what did it matter if Dorrie enjoyed her father's attention?

Father preached a brief sermon on God's faithfulness in sparing them from disaster in the fire and in bringing them back to this place of worship.

"And now for the final act of dedication."

Father's words made Anna sit up straight. They had gone through the program many times and it was to end now.

Colby plunked Dorrie to Anna's lap and hurried down the aisle.

She couldn't imagine where he went in such a hurry, then her attention was diverted by a murmur at the back and she turned to see what caused the disturbance.

Before she could see any cause, uncertain voices began to sing, "Amazing grace, how sweet the sound." The song, sung in deep male voices without instrumental accompaniment, drew her attention to the door.

A parade of men entered, a cross over their shoulders.

Anna recognized the men as those who had been in and out of the church the past month. They still wore shabby clothes but their faces glowed as they marched up the aisle carrying the cross. Colby was the last man in line.

She swallowed hard as they stepped to the platform and lowered the cross. They turned it for all to see and she gasped. The original cross, scarred by the fire, formed the center of a new one, blending seamlessly into the new structure.

Colby cleared his throat. "The cross is scarred. As it should be. I don't think it was a thing of beauty so much as a crude rough instrument of torture on which my Savior died. He died for all of us here. You, me and these men standing with me. Each of us on this stage has found mercy and forgiveness at the foot of an old rugged cross. Not this one. This is only a reminder. But at the cross upon which Jesus died. However, I know some people have found comfort from looking at this reminder of God's love."

He glanced at Anna and flashed a quick smile.

She could barely see him through the sheen of tears.

"My hope and prayer is that many more of you will find comfort, mercy and forgiveness at the cross."

He signaled the men and they hung the cross on the back wall.

"Have you noticed the border?" Colby asked the audience.

Anna scrubbed her eyes so she could see clearly. An intricately carved design formed a beautiful border.

"You can't see it from where you sit but this border is names, dates and verses. These men have come to the Lord and this is their testimony of salvation."

He nodded and one by one the men stepped to the cross and touched a place.

"Slink, May 25. 'For by grace are ye saved.'"

"Tobias, May 26. 'For God so loved the world.'"

"Luke, June 1. 'He gave the right to become children of God.'"

By the time all the men said their names and read their verses, tears trickled down Anna's cheeks. She heard others sniffing and wondered if there could be a dry eye in the place.

Colby went to the cross. "Colby, May 20. 'If any man be in Christ, he is a new creature.'"

Joy flowed with Anna's tears. God had changed Colby. She needed no further proof. She gladly, willingly trusted him.

He met her eyes across the space of the platform and smiled. *For you.* She heard the silent words.

He'd done this for her. He'd repaired the cross so she could remember the times she'd found strength. It was a wonderful gift, blessing her and others, as well.

The men paraded back down the aisle. As they passed, many reached out from the pews to shake their hands. Colby followed them out.

Anna had to wait for the others to depart before she could make it outside. She wanted to find Colby but the crowd kept them apart.

Mr. Steves sat in the place of honor. A big slab of birthday cake practically filled the table in front of him. People filed by extending best wishes as they made their way past to secure a place at one of the benches.

She tried to find Colby in the crowd, caught his eyes across the yard before someone stepped into her path. She shifted, searched for him where she'd last seen him but he had moved. She saw him to one side.

He tipped his chin, signaling her to stay there. He headed in her direction, weaving in and out of the people who crowded around for a chance to speak to Mr. Steves.

She stood watching as he closed the distance between them, her joy mounting with every moment. God had graciously answered her prayer.

Colby finally made it to Anna's side.

She had so much to tell him but didn't know where to start. "Thank you," she whispered. "The cross is beautiful." She meant so much more but couldn't form a solid thought.

"I'm glad you like it. I hoped you would."

And then the opportunity passed as the crowd sang "Happy Birthday."

Miss Weaver had taken over organizing the tea and when Anna went to the table to help serve, the woman shooed her away.

"You go look after that sweet baby."

So she returned to Colby's side. They sat down, Dorrie between them as the ladies served cake to each and everyone.

She wanted to say more. Find words to describe what she felt but the crowd hushed as the mayor gave a speech. Other dignitaries spoke and Mr. Steves responded with a gracious thank you but Anna hardly heard as she watched Colby feed Dorrie cake. She was consumed with a love so full, so sweet, so surprisingly powerful she could hardly think as longing rose up within her, a need to belong to him wholly and completely, be with him always, sharing the joys of each day, supporting each other through the hard times.

Her heart seemed to swell with every beat until she felt nothing but the emotion of the moment.

The clapping as Mr. Steves finished his speech

startled her. She scrambled to pull her thoughts back to where they belonged—thinking about her responsibilities—as people pressed in around them, some shaking Colby's hand, thanking him for the job on the church or the gift of the cross. Others paused to thank Anna for her song, or ask about washing dishes from the tea.

She directed the cleanup. When she looked up, Colby was gone.

Chapter Fourteen

As Colby followed the men to help set up fireworks he couldn't stop grinning. Anna had been pleased with how he'd fixed the cross. Her eyes glistened when she thanked him. Her gaze seemed to cling to him, following his every move.

He knew she wanted to say more but there was too much commotion. It would have to wait.

Later, his job done, he found Anna sitting on a bench, Dorrie asleep in her arms. The way she smiled up at him, her eyes laced with gladness and welcome, his heart forgot it was supposed to beat regularly. Instead, it hesitated then pulsed blood through his veins with such force he felt it pound against his eardrum. And welcomed the noise.

He sat close to her, stroking Dorrie's damp head. "It's been a big day for her."

"I'm afraid we'll pay for it tomorrow. She doesn't like having her routine changed."

Her breath, soft and alluring, whispered over his cheek. He wanted nothing more than to wrap his arms around this woman who had stolen his heart, and this baby who was flesh of his flesh, to hold them close forever, take care of them, protect them—could he? Or would he fail?

He shoved the doubts away. Tonight was for celebration and joy. He shifted, leaning one elbow on the table as he faced her. "I'll help with her."

The smile in her eyes spoke welcome and home.

Home. What he'd always wanted.

What he dreamed would be possible with sweet Anna and now, as well, his little Dorrie.

They had to talk but not here. Not now when others dashed by or stopped to speak to them. Not with his precious daughter sleeping in Anna's arms.

The light faded.

"Time for the fireworks," he murmured.

The sky lit with flashes. Smoke trailed after the light and a deep-throated thunder followed.

The crowd clapped and cheered.

Dorrie wakened, crying and throwing herself backward.

Colby lifted her from Anna's lap. "Look at the lights. Fireworks."

Another burst filled the sky and Dorrie stopped crying so suddenly she coughed.

The show went on for twenty minutes, then people began to disperse. Someone had lit lanterns along the street to help the crowd find its way to their buggies and wagons.

Dorrie started to fuss.

"Time for bed," Anna said.

"I'll take her in."

Dorrie was inconsolable by the time they made their way to the house.

Anna reached for her. "She won't settle when she's this upset. I'll have to rock her to sleep." She smiled at Colby as she bounced the crying child. "Good night."

He patted Dorrie's head. He didn't want to end the day but Dorrie needed her bed and her mama. "I'll see you tomorrow."

She nodded and left him to find his own way out.

He made his way to the shack he'd been sharing with Tobias. As he opened the door a gangly youth rushed toward him.

"Mr. Bloxham. Mr. Bloxham. I been looking all over for you. Got a telegram. Real important."

Colby rescued the yellow bit of paper the boy waved about and quickly read it. He grunted and scrubbed a hand over his chin.

Tobias watched. "Bad news?"

"I have to go. Take this to Miss Caldwell first thing in the morning."

Anna fell asleep with her lips curved in a smile. Tomorrow she and Colby would find a time and place to talk. All evening she had turned to him, knowing her eyes brimmed with promise and acceptance. His had responded with such joy she found herself overflowing with laughter. Thankfully others seemed to be in a celebratory mood and didn't think her actions inappropriate.

Something jerked her from a sound sleep. Her room was dark. She listened, straining to hear any unusual sound.

The sound came again. A choking cry.

Dorrie! Something about the child's cry sounded terribly wrong.

She raced for the baby's bedroom but even before she stepped through the door she heard the laborious breathing.

Hurrying, she lit the lamp and bent over the crib. It took only a glance to see Dorrie's glassy eyes and flushed cheeks. "Poor baby. No wonder you were fussy."

The first thing she had to do was tackle the fever. No, perhaps she needed to address the breathing first. She raced to the kitchen, threw coal in the stove and put a kettle to boil.

As she waited for it to sing she rushed back to the bedroom, dragged the rocking chair close to the crib and used a sheet to prepare a steam tent. Dorrie would protest but it had to be done.

She raced back for the steaming kettle and a basin that she put on a little stool in front of the chair then picked up Dorrie, moaning at how the little one strained for each breath. She stripped her down to her diaper. She poured the boiling water into the basin, pulled the sheet over them and held Dorrie over the steam.

Sweat soon poured from every pore in Anna's body but she continued to pour in hot water until the kettle was drained.

As soon as the steam cooled, she returned Dorrie to her bed and hurried to get a basin of tepid water. Frantically she set to sponging the child, praying desperately for the fever to subside, for Dorrie's lungs to open.

Dawn spilled pink light over the horizon and Anna saw no improvement. Her worry gave way to fear as real and cruel as a fist to her stomach. "Please, God. Take the fever from her. Ease her breathing."

Alex stumbled sleepy-eyed to the room. "She sick?"

"Yes. Get Father."

He stared at her still half-asleep.

"Hurry."

He suddenly came to life and ran down the hall. A few minutes later Father rushed in. "I can hear her breathing from my bedroom."

She pressed her lips together and struggled to control the sobs tearing at her throat.

Father crossed the room and took her in his arms. "Father in heaven, our Almighty Savior and the Great Physician, please touch Dorrie's body and free her lungs."

Anna shuddered. "I'm afraid."

Father hugged her. "What do you need me to do?"

"Get Colby. He needs to be here."

"I'll go right away." He squeezed her shoulders. "Have faith." Then he hurried out.

She heard the front door close after him. Colby would soon be here. She had never needed him more or wanted him more desperately.

"Alex, get me a bucket of warm water." All night she had alternately sponged Dorrie to reduce the fever and steamed her to ease her breathing.

Alex hurried to do her bidding. He hovered at Dorrie's bedside, his eyes wide, his fear palpable. "She looks so sick. I'm scared."

"Me, too." But her efforts were focused on conquering the fever.

A few minutes later she heard the door open

and close. She turned to face Colby, ready to throw herself into his arms. Ready to accept his help and support in fighting for Dorrie's life.

Father stood there. Alone.

"Where's Colby?" Something must have detained him.

Father's expression filled with regret and sorrow. "He's gone."

"How long will he be?"

"Anna, he's gone. Left. I managed to waken Tobias but he was there alone. He said Colby rode out last night."

Gone. Just like always. And she had trusted him again. Moreover, she and Dorrie needed him. She pressed her fist to her mouth to keep from crying. With great effort she tossed aside her pain and disappointment and turned back to Dorrie. They would manage without him.

She pushed aside the wail that demanded how. How would she survive? Especially if something happened to Dorrie?

She had no one but herself to blame for believing him.

For a moment she fought for control. She'd done this before. She could do it again.

"I'm sorry," Father said.

"What time is it?"

"Five."

"Go wake the doctor and tell him he's needed."

The doctor came, said to keep on with what she was doing, and left again, promising to stop in later in the day.

Anna wondered how much longer Dorrie could survive her struggle. Nothing but fighting for Dorrie's life mattered.

She would not think of the pain of Colby leaving again.

The hours slipped by marked by trips to get fresh water, to try and dribble a few drops into Dorrie's parched mouth, to steam her until Anna felt like a pile of runny mashed potatoes.

She was vaguely aware of others coming and going, bringing her water or towels or a drink for herself and Dorrie. She knew the doctor stopped in again and then night fell and she was alone.

But she would not think.

Not of Colby leaving nor of the possibility of losing Dorrie.

"You have to get better, sweetie," she urged and redoubled her efforts to fight the fever, get Dorrie's lungs open.

Morning came unnoticed until Alex and Father slipped into the room, their faces revealing a worry that matched her own.

Again the doctor came by. He shook his head. "If she doesn't turn around soon…"

Anna gave him a look of disdain. "She will." She had to.

Father returned some time later. "Miss Weaver is here."

Grace stepped into the room. "I'm here to help. Now you go rest."

"I couldn't. What if…?"

Grace put her arm around Anna. "You must take care of yourself or who will take care of Dorrie when she's better?"

Anna could have hugged her for saying that and allowed herself to be drawn away. "You'll waken me if…"

"Trust me. I will get you at any change."

So weary she could barely take off her shoes, Anna fell to her bed. Colby had said the same words. Trust me. *Oh, Colby, where are you? Why must you leave me every time I need you desperately?*

"Anna, wake up. Hurry." Father shook her.

"Dorrie?" Was it bad news?

She bolted from her bed and almost fell to the floor as her knees turned to pudding. Clinging to Father's arm she hurried to Dorrie's room.

Dorrie lay on the narrow cot in the corner of the room so still Anna couldn't detect any sign of breathing.

Grace sat on a chair at her side, her look so full of sorrow that Anna cried out a protest. Every organ in her body spasmed with incredible pain.

Then Dorrie sucked in a raspy breath, her chest drawing in cruelly as she fought to get air into her lungs.

Anna fell to her knees beside the cot and cradled her arms around Dorrie's hot little body.

Grace smoothed her hand over Anna's back. "She's fighting very hard."

"She can't die. She can't. I won't let her. God can't take her from me." She stopped the words that poured forth.

Father patted her back. "Anna, don't blame God for our losses."

"Who can I blame?"

"Death is just part of life."

She rolled her head back and forth in denial. "Not untimely death."

Grace pressed a hand to Anna's head. "Nothing can separate us from God's love. In the dark times we learn to trust Him most and find His comfort sweetest."

Father continued to pat her back. "God loves us. We just need to trust Him."

Anna buried her face in the quilt covering the cot and clamped her lips together. Father would be shocked at the words flooding her mind. But what kind of loving God took away those she cared about? He could have stopped Colby from leaving. He could have prevented Rose and Timmy from dying. And He could, if He chose, heal Dorrie. Her fists curled into the fabric at Dorrie's side and she hung on. She would not let this child go. God could not have her. Her teeth clenched so hard it sent a pain straight to the top of her head but she would not let go. Never.

Dorrie shuddered.

Anna's throat clogged with a rush of emotion. She lifted her head. Tears stung the back of her eyes but she would not let them escape.

Dorrie lay quiet and still. Peaceful even. Was she gone? Hot floodwaters of grief swept through her, grabbing at her heart with vicious fingers, sucking at her limbs as she fought the undercurrent threatening to drown her. She wouldn't fight anymore. She'd simply let the waters wash her away.

Dorrie coughed.

Anna jumped, startled by the unexpected sound. Was it the last dying response? She placed her hand on Dorrie's chest. *My baby. My baby. How can I go on without your sweet presence?* She opened her mouth and closed it again and again as if she could pump out her overwhelming sorrow.

The little chest beneath her palm rose and fell.

She stared at her hand. Had she imagined it? No. It rose and fell again. "She's breathing." Her words were barely a whisper. "She's breathing." Anna jumped to her feet, laughing and crying. "She's breathing."

She hugged Father. "She's breathing."

Father's face was wet with tears. "Praise God. Praise God."

Anna turned to Grace. "She's breathing. She's alive."

Grace, her eyes glittering with tears, hugged Anna. "God has blessed your faith."

Her faith? She'd had none. Only doubts and anger. Why had she not trusted God? Shame crackled at the edge of her joy.

The doctor came, proclaimed it a wonder that Dorrie had turned a corner toward getting well.

Dorrie was alive. Her breathing rattled but at last filled her lungs.

She lived. Anna's joy knew no end even though she didn't deserve it. When she should have trusted, she doubted. But thanks to God, He hadn't punished her lack of faith.

Dorrie was weak and listless. Anna had her hands full caring for her in the following days and welcomed Grace's help running the home.

She gratefully cared for Dorrie, finding unlimited patience with her fussiness.

But in the pit of her stomach lay a boulder of guilt. Hadn't she learned to trust God at a young age? Wasn't it trust that bore her through those dark days of sorrow when Rose and Timmy died?

Who was she that she could forget God's faithfulness when she needed it most?

Grace spent a few hours each day helping with meals. She had left for the day with supper in the oven saying she needed to help her sister.

Anna sat at the table holding Dorrie, tenderly spooning warm porridge into her.

The door burst open without so much as a knock and Colby stood with the light behind him.

Anna blinked. "What are you doing here? How long are you around for this time?" She felt no welcome. No gladness. Only a long dark ache. Why did he keep riding in and out of her life? How much more could she take?

"I came as soon as I heard. As soon as I got back."

Anna returned her attention to Dorrie, ignoring Colby. They'd said it all before. Nothing had changed. Nothing had been resolved.

Colby crossed the room in two strides and knelt at her side. "Oh, Dorrie, my poor little girl." His voice thickened as he stroked her face.

"Da-da," Dorrie croaked and gave a crooked smile.

He lifted his head to look at Anna. "Was it very hard?"

She didn't answer, only gave him a disinterested shrug.

"I wish I had been here."

"Seems you have the habit of leaving just when things get tough."

Cradling Dorrie's hands in his, Colby sat back on his heels. "You read the telegram. You know where I went."

She snorted. "I saw no telegram."

"Tobias was supposed to give it to you." He watched her face and saw her obvious denial then sighed. "I should have known better than to expect him to remember. Anna, I didn't leave."

She turned away, resumed feeding Dorrie.

"Listen to me. Remember that letter I wrote to my friend Hugh?"

He waited but she gave no indication whether or not she did. But of course she did.

"I got a telegram from the sheriff telling me Hugh had been injured and I was to come immediately if I wanted to see him before he died."

A little spark of sympathy flickered in the depths of her solitude. "I'm sorry."

Colby grinned. "He didn't die. I made sure of that. Brought him back with me. He's recuperating in one of the hotel rooms right now."

She nodded, continued feeding Dorrie.

"Don't you understand, Anna? I didn't leave. I only went to help a friend."

"I see." But nothing inside her cared. She couldn't take any more leaving or worrying about him leaving.

When he asked, she let him hold Dorrie and feed her. She let him stay to tuck her into bed. She let him kneel at her crib and pray.

But she could not let him into her heart.

Colby knelt in the church and poured out his heart to God. He'd been back several days. He rejoiced to see Dorrie daily growing stronger. But Anna had shut herself up inside solid fort walls and would not let him near. Not that he could blame her. She had every reason to doubt him.

Just as he doubted himself.

He had failed so many times. He'd failed to protect his mother. He'd failed to protect Nora. He'd failed his friends. He'd failed Anna over and over.

Getting to Hugh and helping was the one time he'd managed to make a step toward undoing the damage he'd done.

But would he ever be able to undo the harm he'd done with Anna? Did he have anything to offer her or would he, when push came to shove, fail her in a big way?

Part of him considered leaving now, before she could be more greatly disappointed in him.

But he was through running from his fears and failures. With God's help.

A little later he stepped into the glaring sunlight, mounted his horse and rode toward the hotel to check on Hugh who grew stronger each day. He planned to be back at the Caldwell house when Dorrie woke from her nap so he could feed her and hold her. To think this precious child had almost died. It filled his heart with praise that God had chosen to spare her.

When he arrived at the house, Grace was there. "Now here's Colby," she said to Anna. "Let him take you for a walk." She turned to Colby. "She needs to get outside. Get some fresh air before she gets sick, too."

Here was the chance Colby had prayed for. "Can't have you getting sick. Who would look after everyone?" He reached for her hand, tucked it around his elbow and was out the door before she could protest.

She jerked free. "I don't want to go for a walk."

"Do it for Dorrie." She sure could be stubborn.

"Fine." Anna faced forward and marched down the street as if ordered to the gallows.

Colby kept pace. "Look, Anna. I know you're angry with me. I know you've been through a lot with Dorrie. I can't imagine how scared you must have been but—"

"Please let me enjoy the fresh air."

Colby sighed. She was so distant and unreachable. "Don't you know it hurts me to know I wasn't here when you and Dorrie needed me? I would never have gone after Hugh if I'd known."

She nodded briskly without turning her attention from the path before her. "Good to know."

"I never thought to see you so bitter."

That made her stop and face him, her eyes flaring with an emotion that he could not identify. "I am not bitter."

"Sure could fool me."

"I'm—" She shook her head. "I'm not bitter."

Maybe if she met Hugh she would understand. Hugh had said he might venture out into the sunshine. He directed their steps toward the hotel and smiled when he saw Hugh tipped back in one of the chairs on the boardwalk in front of the hotel.

"There's my friend. Let's say hello." She made no protest as they crossed the distance between them. He made the introductions.

"Pleased to meet you, ma'am," Hugh said. "Did this here man tell you how he saved my life?"

Chapter Fifteen

Anna nodded. Hugh was clean-shaven, wore clean clothes, had his foot swathed in heavy bandages, and sported bruises and cuts on his face and hands. "Looks like you might have lost a war."

Hugh chuckled. "Got run over by a loaded wagon. Would have died if Colby hadn't shown up and forced me to get better." He shifted his amused glance to Colby. "Maybe forcing that old quack of a doctor to show a little mercy helped, too."

"I owed you."

Hugh and Colby stared at each other, sharing some secret.

"If you ever owed me the debt is paid."

Anna shifted her gaze from one to the other and when neither seemed about to share any details, she decided to press for more. "What's this debt thing?"

Colby shook his head and shot Hugh a look rife with warning but Hugh ignored him. "I saved his hide a time or two. One time especially that he's referring to—"

"Anna, let's get back. I want to feed Dorrie."

Anna shook off his hand. "In a minute." Hugh knew something and she wanted to find out what. Perhaps it would explain what had sent Colby running again.

"He kind of went downhill after Nora died."

Anna rolled her eyes at the understatement and Hugh chuckled.

"Yeah, you're right. He fell into a hole. A deep hole."

Colby made a dissenting noise and tried to turn Anna toward home.

She shied away. "So what happened?"

"You mean besides the drinking and carousing?"

She nodded, assuming there was more.

"One night he decided it was the doctor's fault Nora died and he headed out to kill the man. I think he would have if I hadn't stopped him."

Anna gasped and stared at Colby. "Is that true?" She couldn't imagine him a murderer. "You would have hung."

"I was drunk. As soon as I sobered up, I left."

That explained a lot.

"Now can we go?" He waved an arm down the street and gave her an expectant look that said it was time.

She fell in beside him, her mind flooded with questions. "Why did you blame the doctor? He did the best he could." She remembered how she felt when Dorrie was so sick. "Never mind. I know how frustrated I was that he could do nothing when Dorrie almost died."

"I didn't really blame him." He sounded weary—soul weary.

Her heart went out to him. He'd lost his wife. He'd been left with an infant daughter to care for. And he had no one. At least she had her father and brother when Rose died. And later, she'd baby Dorrie to tend to. She'd been so busy with the baby she had little time for Colby. Nor patience with his drinking.

Colby went on in low tones. "It was just easier to blame him then blame myself."

"Why would you blame anyone?" Birthing babies was difficult work. Women often died doing it.

"'Cause it was my job to make sure she was safe. And I didn't."

He confused her. "How can you be responsible for things out of your control? I don't understand."

He pushed out a noisy gust of air. "Guess it's a man thing."

She considered the idea. True, men and women had different roles. Women typically cared for the home and children. Men…she'd never considered their role and she did so now. And, yes, perhaps they were expected to provide and protect. So when things went wrong, things out of their control, did they feel they had failed? It was a new thought. "I don't think anyone has the right to blame a man if he encounters things beyond his control. Even things that threaten his family."

"Seems there is always something a person could do."

"Like what?"

"Something."

She understood he felt powerless and hated it. Maybe rather than face his inability to change things, he left. "Colby, why did you leave your home?"

"What home?"

"With your father. I know he beat you but why did you leave?"

"Because I couldn't stop him from hurting Ma." The words burst forth as if shot from a canon. "It made my ma leave. I couldn't stop it."

She ground to a halt and faced him. His fist clenched into knots. His face creased into sorrowful lines. "You were a kid."

"I wanted to stop him. I couldn't."

"So you left."

"Comes a time a person can't look at himself in the mirror."

She wondered how many times he would see his reflection, not like what he saw and leave. She wasn't about to pin any hopes on his staying.

Colby jerked to a halt and almost stumbled.

She watched the color drain from his face. And then he blinked and pulled his hat lower. She turned to see what caused this reaction. Didn't seem to be anything out of the ordinary except a stranger riding down the street—a big man with an unfriendly turn to his mouth.

He drew closer and pulled his horse toward them to glower at Colby. Then he shifted to study Anna with such intensity her face burned.

The air crackled with tension. Anna held her breath, wondering what this man wanted with them.

He gave a mocking smile. "Colby. You look a mite surprised."

"I thought you were dead."

"I don't die as easy as you hoped."

Anna's tongue stuck to the sides of her mouth. She struggled to focus her thoughts. Colby knew this man?

Colby grabbed her elbow and steered her toward home. She lurched along at his side.

"Be seeing you 'round," the man called after them.

They were almost at the manse when Anna jerked away to face him. "Who was that?"

"Lew. Someone from my past."

"Why did you think he was dead?"

"Never mind." He hurried on, urging her forward.

There was something sinister and wicked about that Lew fella. He knew Colby too well for comfort. Was he one of Colby's associates? What did he want here? Had he come to persuade Colby to ride away with him?

She almost tripped and Colby grabbed her elbow to steady her. She yanked back her arm and confronted him. "Just when I thought I was beginning to understand what makes you tick…" Would she never get past an endless hope that this time, perhaps now, he would stay and be the man she needed? Her heart turned to coal. "Just make sure he stays away from Dorrie." She forced her wooden legs into the house and closed the door to lean against it, praying she wouldn't collapse.

Grace stepped from the kitchen. "You're back." She sprang forward. "What happened? You look like you're going to be ill."

"I guess I'm more worn out than I realized." She straightened, hoping her quivering knees would not fail her. She knew Colby had been involved in unsavory things while he was away. She'd heard plenty of tales about his wild escapades. But she never thought to encounter that sort of man because of him.

She wanted so badly to believe he'd changed that she looked for nothing but proof.

Oh, Lord. Protect us from his friends. Protect my heart.

It was too late for her heart. Had always been too late. She'd loved him since she was fourteen. She knew beneath that rough exterior, beyond his shameful past, lay a Colby full of tenderness and understanding. Unfortunately his past seemed too full to overcome, his exterior too tough. Yet—her faith protested—wasn't God able to do a work in his life? What was the verse Grace had mentioned in her debate with Mrs. Percy? "He who has begun a good work in you will complete it." She'd pray for God to complete His work in Colby's life. Make him able to resist whatever pull this man from his past had on him. Stay and be the kind of father Dorrie needed.

And she'd confine her thoughts to that. No more. She could not, would not, let herself care about him as anything more than Dorrie's father.

She stepped into the kitchen where Dorrie sat picking at some bread and butter. *Oh, Dorrie. How can I keep you safe?* That man, that friend of Colby's, frightened her. She wanted to grab Dorrie and hold her close.

Colby's thoughts went round and round. He'd left Lew and Harv and everything they stood for behind. He hoped Anna would never learn of what he'd been, what he'd done. Now Lew was here. But where was Harv?

He got his horse and rode through town. Rode a mile or two in each direction. But he saw no sign of Lew. Perhaps the man had moved on. But the thought gave him no comfort. Lew had come for a purpose. Likely revenge. After all, a man wasn't expected to like being shot.

No, Lew would be back.

Colby had taken part-time work at the feed store and headed that direction where he spent several hours. Normally he enjoyed the way work made thinking unnecessary, but today he found no such respite from his thoughts.

He knew the depravity of Lew's heart.

And he feared for Anna and Dorrie.

Might be best for them if he rode out this day, but unless he could be certain Lew followed hard on his heels, Colby would not be leaving Anna and Dorrie unprotected.

Suppertime came and Colby shared the meal

with Hugh. He told Hugh about Lew. Telling the story only increased his restlessness.

He pushed back from the table. "I have to check on Anna and the baby. Make sure they're okay."

He rode over. Circled the house. Picked his way down the trail by the river but saw no sign of Lew. His absence only made Colby more concerned. Better Lew out in the open then Lew sneaking about where Colby couldn't watch him.

Still uneasy he returned to his quarters. Twice more before dark he rode out to check on things. No Lew. But at least Anna and Dorrie were safe inside the four solid walls of the house.

The next morning, he was up early and out to repeat his rounds. He came on signs of a campfire near where he had stayed by the river. The ashes were still warm. Could be anyone but he was convinced it was Lew.

Much as he wanted to stop in and see Anna and Dorrie, he dare not. The less Lew saw of where he went and who he saw, the better for all concerned.

Poor Mr. Rawlings must have wondered at Colby that day. He excused himself so often to ride down the street and check on Anna the man would be starting to think Colby didn't intend to put in a full day's work. Or even a reasonable portion of a day.

Once he saw Anna crossing between the house

and the church. She glanced his direction, saw it was him, paused a moment then hurried into the shelter of the building.

He couldn't blame her for her caution.

For two days he stayed away. And in those two days he saw little clues that suggested Lew was about—a bit of rag tied to the tree across from the manse, another warm campfire, an *X* slashed into the door Colby went in and out as he did his work for Mr. Rawlings.

The third day he informed his boss he wouldn't be in to work. He planned to find Lew and settle whatever score the man felt needed to be settled.

Anna peeked through the window. That man was there. Lew. He flitted in and out of sight throughout the day, always watching the house. She dared not step outside.

"Father, he's there again."

Father joined her at the window. "You say he's a friend of Colby's?"

"I think *friend* might be too generous a word."

Father watched a moment then Lew slid out of sight. "Is there any reason he is watching us?"

"Not that I'm aware."

"It's not the way I expect a man to act. Perhaps you should refrain from going outside unless you have someone with you. Preferably myself or Colby."

But Colby did not come anymore. She'd seen him ride by a few times but he always passed without any indication of stopping. She thought of waving him in or shouting a greeting but something stopped her. She couldn't say if it was caution, fear or anger. Perhaps a bit of all three.

Under the circumstances how could he expect her to trust him? She didn't know what was going on and he didn't choose to tell her.

She turned from the window but glanced out every few minutes. It seemed better to know when Lew was watching them then to wonder if he was.

The next time she glanced out, she saw Colby stop at the side of the road. Lew stood in the shadows and grinned mockingly as Colby dismounted. Then they disappeared into the trees.

Now was her chance to find out what was going on. Dorrie lay sleeping in her crib. Anna could safely steal away and follow the men. She stepped outside. Had to hurry or she might lose them or miss whatever was about to transpire. She picked up her skirts and ran. As soon as she entered the shelter of the trees and the coolness of the shade they provided, she slowed to allow her eyes a chance to adjust to the change in light. Ahead, she heard the murmur of voices and carefully avoided stepping on any twigs as she crept forward, her heart clinging to the back of her throat with a grip of steel.

She saw Colby first, probably because she knew she would not be able to draw in a breath until she knew he was safe.

He stood, thumbs hooked in the front pockets of his trousers. The stance was likely intended to look casual, unconcerned, but Anna saw tension in the way he balanced on the balls of his feet and how his shoulders crunched toward his ears. Colby was alert in every muscle.

She shifted her gaze to Lew. The man wore a cruel, mocking scowl.

"Where is it?" Lew growled.

"Where's Harv? Ask him." Colby spoke with careful patience, which only served to make Anna's muscles knot. Colby didn't trust this man. That was obvious.

"Harv's dead. You might say he met with an unfortunate accident."

"You shot him?"

"Couldn't be helped. The man wasn't about to share his information. But you and him were pretty cozy. I figure he told you."

"He didn't."

Lew growled. "'Fraid I don't believe you. I should shoot you here like you deserve." He edged his hands toward the gun hanging low at his side.

Anna bit her bottom lip to keep from crying out. Was she about to see Colby shot dead? Would she never get a chance to tell him she loved him? Her knees threatened to melt and she swayed against a tree for support.

"With both me and Harv dead you'd never find out."

Lew considered the idea, and then slowly his hands left his gun belt. "Guess maybe you're right."

Anna backed away. She managed to stifle her shock until she reached the shelter of her home. She dashed into her room and threw herself across the bed, her heart racing so fast it tore at her chest, sending pain radiating through her body. It sounded as though Colby meant to ride away with that despicable man. When would this ever stop hurting? How much more could she take?

Colby knew there was no money. Harv had led the men to believe there was in order to make them obey his orders. A treasure. Money. Lots of it. Hidden in a safe place. He'd take them there. But first they had to…whatever scheme Harv dreamed up.

To start with, Colby had gone along with Harv's plans, not realizing Harv had bigger, badder things in mind.

But one day Lew had grown more belligerent and challenging than usual. Said he took exception to the growing closeness between Colby and Harv.

Not that there was any friendship. Harv simply liked playing the men off against each other.

Colby's association with them had ended when he shot Lew. Thought he'd killed the man. No loss to society and nobody would dispute it was self-defense, but as Colby stared at the bleeding man, then considered his pistol, he saw what he was becoming and didn't much care for what he saw.

He'd turned around. Headed home. Back to Anna and his baby. Back to where he'd left his heart.

He thought he could escape his past. But his past had caught up with him.

For now he was safe having led Lew to believe he knew the whereabouts of the fake treasure. But not for long. Lew had never been patient.

But it would ensure that Lew followed him out of town and a good long ways from Anna and Dorrie. What would he do when Lew realized there was no stash of money…

Well, he'd deal with that when the time came.

First he must tell Anna he was leaving.

It would be the hardest task he'd ever taken on. Just when he hoped and prayed he'd begun to prove she could trust him not to run off, he had to do it again.

This time there would be no coming back.

But he couldn't let her guess that.

He followed after Lew, waiting for him to ride up to the Lucky Lady and saunter in for a drink. No chance the man would leave until he got what he'd come for—the non-existent money and, after that, revenge for Colby shooting him.

Hard to believe the man had survived. But he was too mean to die easily.

Rather than follow Lew inside, he slowly made his way back to Anna's and the end of his dreams. He would have to be careful when he hugged Dorrie, or Anna would be suspicious. His insides bled worse than Lew had after being shot. He would never see Dorrie grow up but at least she'd be safe and well cared for with Anna.

Anna. He dare not think any further. Just her name in his thoughts was enough to make him weaken.

But he must do what was necessary. He'd failed so many people in the past—his mother, Nora, Hugh, Anna, Dorrie….

He would not, must not, fail this time.

But he didn't go directly to the manse. He rode down a back trail, tied his horse out of sight of the house and slipped into the church. He could not face this alone.

His knees were difficult to bend, stiffened with regret and resolve, but he forced them to obey and knelt before the cross.

When he found sufficient strength, he rose and went next door.

Anna and Dorrie were in the kitchen. He paused at the door to take in each detail—the cupboard where he had helped Dorrie wash dishes, the stove where he didn't even have to close his eyes to picture Anna busy cooking, the table where they had shared so many meals. At last he let his gaze touch the two he loved with his whole heart.

Dorrie's color was almost back to normal after her illness. Her energy increased every day. He smiled at her greeting, *Da-da.* Let his gaze linger on her hair, her blue eyes so much like his.

Last—his heart kicking against his ribs—he let himself look at Anna, the woman he had loved for so long. He wanted to smile, prove to her there was nothing amiss, but at the demanding look in her eyes, he faltered. Had she guessed why he'd come? Already prepared to be angry about it?

"Anna." He paused. How did he convince her without alarming her? "I have to leave."

"You're going with that man aren't you?"

"Lew. Yes. We have some unfinished business."

"Why not leave it unfinished? Is it so important? More important than me? Than Dorrie?"

"No. Never. Nothing is more important than you. But this is for your good." He couldn't tell her the particulars. She would protest. Might even try and stop him. And he must go. It was the only way to protect them and put an end to this.

"What do you have that Lew wants?"

He stilled his face to remain blank but her question caught him off guard. "Unfinished business."

"Who is he? Why does it matter so much what he wants?" If he didn't hear the cry behind her harsh words, he might have thought she was angry.

He took a step forward but she put up her hand to stall him.

"Can't you at least tell me what's going on?"

He wanted to. He wanted to share every detail of his life with her. But would she understand? Would the knowledge somehow increase her risk?

"Colby, I think I deserve to know."

"Very well, but it's not a pretty story." He sat at the table, plopped his hat in front of him and considered where to start.

"You asked why I ran and I told you I was afraid I couldn't be what you needed. That's the truth. I told you I failed my ma. That's the truth. But there's more. Anna, I can never seem to protect the ones I love." Except this time he intended to no matter the cost. A cruel, sharp blade tore through his insides but he gritted his teeth. He would not let her know how much it hurt to do this.

"Lew is one of the men I fell in with when I was away." He told her how Lew and Harv, and others before them, had welcomed him. How he'd done the things they did, rowdy, drunken things. "I didn't like what I was doing but I didn't believe I could change. After all, I am a Bloxham."

"Change is God's business."

He wondered if she truly believed it or simply repeated familiar words. Not that it mattered anymore. "I shot Lew."

She gasped.

"Left him for dead."

Her eyes grew wider. The pain in his heart grew more vicious.

"Self-defense, it was. But that's when I decided I didn't care what it took. I did not like who or what I was becoming."

"That's when you came back here?"

"I came back to you and Dorrie. I came to start over."

She swallowed hard as if trying to get down something hard and bulky. "Then stay. Stay and start over."

He would not blink. He would not groan. Instead he would rejoice that he heard the words he longed for. He would carry them in his heart until his death. "I can't stay. Trust me when I say this is for the best."

He rose, determination warring with a longing that ached through his entire bloodstream and touched every cell of his body. One more day. He'd give anything for one more day. But he dare not tempt Lew to violence.

He stroked Dorrie's hair. Kissed both her cheeks and hugged her. He longed to scoop her out of the chair and hold her forever. But if he showed any unusual degree of emotion, Anna might grow suspicious.

Then he turned to Anna, drinking in every detail. He would hold this picture of her in his mind until the end. "I have to go." He bent and gently kissed her. He planned to make it short and quick but it would be his one and only kiss and he could not force himself away. He gently pulled her close wanting to hold her forever in his arms.

After her initial surprise she leaned into him, wrapped her arms about his waist and returned his kiss.

From somewhere deep inside he found the strength to slowly, reluctantly, ease back. He squeezed her shoulders and stepped away from her embrace. "Take good care of my Dorrie."

He rushed for escape before he weakened.

But before he reached the handle, the door flew back and Lew stood in the opening, his pistol drawn.

Chapter Sixteen

"Well, well. Ain't this sweet?" The man's voice had a sinister leer to it.

Colby positioned himself between Lew and the other two. "I'm ready to go. My horse is outside. I'll take you to the money."

"I do believe you will."

Colby edged forward, cautiouslike, so as not to make Lew consider doing something stupid.

"Hold up there. What's to stop this pretty little gal from running to the sheriff as soon as I leave?"

It's exactly what she should do. "She won't. Will you, Anna?"

"Not if you say I shouldn't."

Good girl. Let's lead him along.

Lew snorted. "You don't expect me to believe that, now do ya?"

Lew could be way too smart sometimes. "You can trust her. After all, she's the preacher's daughter."

"Better she and the baby come along. Provide me a bit of insurance in case you think you can play me for the fool. Lady, pick up that baby and get yourself over here."

He waved the gun.

Colby considered his options. He'd go for the gun but too risky with Dorrie and Anna so close. He'd have to trust God to provide an opportunity before they left town. "Do as he says, Anna."

He hoped she wouldn't decide this was a good time to reveal her stubborn nature. He knew only momentary relief as she clutched Dorrie in her arms and headed for the door.

Lew stepped aside and waved the three of them out.

Colby tried to position himself between Lew and Anna, but Lew would have none of it. "Keep to one side."

"Just keep walking," Colby murmured to Anna.

"That's right, lady. No funny stuff or someone dies."

Colby knew he would not fire his gun in town because it would bring people running to investigate. He prayed for an opening, for Lew to be careless just one second, but the man had unfaltering concentration when he wanted it. And right now with the hope of discovering a fake treasure, he had lots of reason to keep focused.

Three horses were tied at the shed. Lew indicated they should head that way. They reached the mounts. "You first." He shoved Anna forward.

Colby saw at once that she couldn't get in the saddle while holding Dorrie. He stepped forward to help and stopped as Lew's gun bore down on him.

"I'll take the little sweetheart."

"No." Anna jerked back. "I'll not give her to you." Before Colby could shout a warning, Anna turned on her heel and ran for all she was worth toward the church. He understood she hoped to reach shelter before Lew could stop her.

"Fool woman." Lew turned and steadied the gun on Anna.

He intended to shoot her. Maybe Dorrie, too.

"No." Colby launched himself between Lew and Anna and made a few steps before as a shot rang out. The bullet caught him in his back, pushing him forward. But when he fell, he took Anna and Dorrie with him. At least he could protect them with his body.

The pain turned the edges of his vision red but he was alive. For how long, he didn't know. "Are you hurt?"

"No." Her words were muffled by the weight of his body but he wouldn't have moved if he could. He was a shield for them.

"Is Dorrie hurt?"

Dorrie's wail informed them she was at least alive.

"Don't move. Make him either come here or ride away."

Behind them Lew cursed. "Now see what you made me do."

Anna turned her head, tried to see him. "Are you shot?"

"At least I could protect you and Dorrie. Now be quiet and lie still." Every word thundered through his brain, every move she made drove the pain deeper.

Footsteps thundered down the alley. Men called out. "It came from this direction."

Then more gunshots rang out.

"I love you," he managed to squeeze out, and then all went black.

An explosive sound had made her ears ring. She was certain Lew had shot his gun. Her heart slammed into her ribs so hard she felt her ribs crack. Then Colby's weight had hit her hard. Anna fell facedown to the ground, dirt filling her nose, dry grass scratching her cheeks, Dorrie clutched to her. Instinctively she'd shifted the baby to one side to protect her from Anna's weight.

She spat out dirt and grass. "I smell blood." Metallic and sweet.

Colby moaned, "He shot me."

Colby! Hurt. Panic swirled around her. Would the man shoot her, too? What about Dorrie? The child was pressed solidly to her side, pinned in place by Anna's arm. She struggled to shift her arm, somehow protect Dorrie more but she couldn't move and her aching ribs struggled for air.

Colby's ragged breath blew hot on her neck.

She tried to squirm from under his weight.

"Lie still. This here is the safest place you could be." His words rumbled from his body, reverberated in her own.

She stopped struggling.

"I love you." His words came on a whisper and then the weight of his body became intolerable.

"Colby," she whispered.

He didn't answer. She no longer felt his breath on her neck. Colby. Her fear crawled up her skin and pooled against her protesting ribs. "Don't you dare die."

He loved her. Now was a fine time to say so. Why had he waited so long to speak the words?

Would she have believed them any sooner? How could she be so blind not to see how much he loved her? He'd give his life for her. Yet she'd stubbornly refused to trust him. Demanded proof when she should have simply welcomed his return and believed him.

And not just him.

She'd found it so hard to trust God. Always she asked herself, would God take her loved ones, would He do what was best for her or was she simply there for the good of others?

Colby was willing to die for her.

Jesus had done so.

Trust should be easier.

It would be from here on.

Colby? Was her trust too late? Hot tears scalded her face and muddied the ground until she lay in a puddle. *Please, God, don't let him die. Please.* Now was the time to put her faith into action. *I trust You to do what is best.*

More gunshots rang out. Anna cringed, fearing she would feel one thud into Colby's inert body. She tried to pull Dorrie closer but the weight of Colby's body made it impossible. She struggled to get in enough air to keep from blacking out.

Then voices spoke above her. "Here, give me a hand."

Slowly, Colby's body was lifted. Someone called, "Get the doc."

Another set of hands started to take Dorrie.

Anna fought.

"Let me take her." It was Grace.

She released her grip and Dorrie was lifted. She realized Dorrie was sobbing. How long had she been crying and Anna didn't notice? Didn't hear?

She wanted to flip over but her limbs had no strength. Her lungs fought to get air. Someone gently turned her and helped her sit. "Father." She buried her head against his chest and wailed. "I've been so stupid and blind." It hurt her lungs to squeeze out the words.

"Shush. Shush." He patted her back, offering her comfort in a way he had never before. "You've just had a terrible shock."

She jerked from his arms. "Where is that man? Lew?" She glanced around, her eyes burning with dread. Was he still lurking about, waiting for a chance to finish this business between him and Colby?

"He was shot trying to escape. He's dead."

Anna tried to feel sorrow at a senseless death but felt only relief that he wouldn't terrorize them again.

"Colby?" She tried to get to her feet. Again her body would not do as she ordered. "Is he—?" She couldn't say the word.

"They've rushed him over to Doc's place. He'll do what he can."

"He's still alive?" She had to know the truth.

"I heard someone say he was breathing."

She moaned and fell back into Father's arms. "Please pray he doesn't die."

"Of course. I already am. Now let's have a look at you. Are you injured?"

"I'm fine." Only it took Father on one side and Mr. Percy on the other for her to make it to the house. They helped her to her bedroom and left her to Grace's care.

Grace brought in water and tenderly washed Anna's face. Anna lay with her eyes closed, too weak to even protest. At first, she wanted to, she should be looking after herself, then she relaxed. Time to stop trying to take care of everything. Not only did she need to trust God and Colby, she needed to let others help her more.

"Thank God you and Dorrie aren't injured. You have a few scratches and no doubt you'll have bruises but nothing serious," Grace said as she cleaned Anna's hands.

Anna tried not to flinch. Her palms must be scratched to hurt so. "Dorrie's all right?"

"I think she was more frightened than anything. Alex is home and he's amusing her. I heard her laugh a few minutes ago."

She and Dorrie had gotten off easy. Unlike Colby. Tears washed her eyes and ran down each side of her face.

Grace made a soothing noise and wiped them away. "Come here." She reached for Anna, urging her into her embrace.

Anna sat up and buried her face against the woman's shoulder. Sobs racked her.

"You go right ahead and have a good cry."

Anna cried like she hadn't cried before. She wept for her fear and regrets over Colby. And her tears carried prayers that he would live, so she could tell him how much she loved him. How much she trusted him. With her life. But she cried for other things, too. Never had she been held and comforted since Rose died. She'd taken all her sorrow to the foot of the cross but now she let warm arms hold her and hot tears cleanse her. She cried until she was spent and Grace's dress front soaked.

"I'm sorry," she mumbled, unable to meet Grace's eyes. The woman must think she was a weak-kneed ninny. She almost smiled. She was certainly weak-kneed at the moment.

Grace chuckled. "Woman-to-woman, let me tell you there is nothing like a weeping session to ease one's emotions. Men don't understand but we do."

Anna grinned, realizing just how right Grace was. She hadn't felt so cleansed in a long time. "Thank you."

"Don't thank me. Thank God who gave us tears. Now you lie down and rest. I'll take care of everything else."

She knew she wouldn't sleep. She intended to stay awake and pray for Colby until she heard one way or the other. But she fell into a deep dreamless sleep as soon as her head hit the pillow.

"Mama?"

Tiny fingers brushed at her face. Anna yawned.

"Dorrie, come away and let her sleep," Alex whispered.

"I'm awake." She moaned. And remembered why everything hurt. She bolted to her feet. And swayed. Grace was right. She ached in places she didn't know existed.

"You sure you should be up?" Alex asked.

"I'm fine." But she sat on the edge of the bed and waited for the dizziness to pass. "Colby?"

"Father," Alex called. "She's awake."

Father was to deliver the news? Fear crept into her throat and made it impossible to swallow. Father's job was to deliver bad news.

Dorrie wanted to be picked up, but Anna didn't think she could lift her, so she patted the bed beside her. Dorrie climbed up and buried her face in Anna's lap. Anna rubbed her back, finding comfort in her nearness. If Colby were gone she would have this sweet bit of him. She pressed her lips to hold back a cry. She didn't want to lose Colby. She'd missed too many precious days already.

Father appeared at the doorway. "How are you feeling?"

"Sore but otherwise fine." She clung to his kind gaze. "Tell me the truth. Is Colby—?"

He sat beside Dorrie and took Anna's hand. "He's alive. But just barely. Doc isn't hopeful."

Alive. That's all that mattered. "Then we'll have to ask God to help him."

Father turned her hand over and seemed to study the many scrapes and scratches. "We need to trust God to do what is best."

What was best was for Colby to live so they could enjoy their love. Raise Dorrie together. She fought an intense battle. She had a choice—trust God or wonder about His love. She'd wasted too much time letting God show His love in areas of her choosing, trusting Him when she got her way. She gripped Father's hand and bowed her head. "Not my will but God's," she murmured.

Father squeezed her shoulder and prayed, "Father, we ask that You see fit to heal Colby, bring him back to us, but in this, as we strive to do in all areas, we release him to You and trust Your good mercy and grace."

Anna sat quietly, her eyes still closed. Great peace filled her. Whatever God sent her way, He would also send the grace to deal with it. And if what He sent was Colby, she would never let another day pass without telling him she loved him.

"Where is he?"

"Doc kept him at his office until he can be moved."

"Who is caring for him?"

"There seems no end to his friends wanting to help. Doc had to chase a bunch of them away. Said they were getting underfoot."

"I want to see him."

Father hesitated. "Are you up to it?"

"He saved my life. I owe him. Besides…"

Father smiled. "I understand your feelings."

She ducked her head, afraid he might see far more than gratitude.

"I'll take you to see him."

"Thank you. Is Grace here?"

"Yes. She said she'll be available as long as we need her."

"Give me a minute to tidy up and then I'll be ready."

She was grateful the doctor's office wasn't any farther away. As it was, she welcomed the way Father tucked her hand around his arm and let her lean on him. The closer they got to their destination, the weaker her legs grew. No matter what happened, she would trust God—with her life, her future—but she ached with unshed tears as she tried to prepare herself for bad news.

They reached Doc's door. Father pushed it open.

Anna stopped. She couldn't step into the room. Couldn't face the news.

Father smiled. "No one has brought a message saying otherwise so I assume he is still fighting to live. Let's go see."

She allowed him to draw her forward. They had to cross a small waiting room where two women sat. Anna was scarcely aware of them except that their murmurs of sympathy increased her tension. *God help me. Be my strength and comfort.*

Doc, having heard the door open and close, stepped into the room, saw Anna and her father. "Come along. The young man is in here."

She somehow crossed the room, her feet numb, and clinging desperately to Father's arm.

"He's lost a lot of blood." Doc spoke with determination. "I had to dig deep for the bullet but he's strong."

Then she saw him and stuffed a fist to her mouth to keep from crying out. He lay on a narrow black bed propped up on one side. A stark white sheet covered the lower half of his body. A huge white dressing wrapped around his right side.

If Father hadn't been holding her arm, she

would have collapsed. He led her to a chair and she sank down.

Slink had vacated the chair and hovered nearby. Tobias sat on the opposite side. He pushed to his feet, nodded politely. "We'll be leaving you alone with him." Both men slipped from the room.

Anna reached out to touch the dressing. Thought better of it and instead took his hand as it lay motionless against the white sheet. "Colby, please get better." Just the feel of his hand gave her courage. He was still alive. That was enough for now.

She looked at his face. Younger-looking with all awareness at rest. And pale. Silently, she prayed for his recovery. Prayed she might get a chance to tell him of her love.

As she sat beside him, she held those three little words he'd spoken—*I love you*—close to her heart. She clung to his hand as faithfully as she clung to hope. And in it all, she felt peace like the rock bed of her life. God would surely do what was best and she would trust Him no matter what.

The hours trudged past as slow as a boy headed off to school on a sunny day. Yet each minute was a chance to see him improve.

Several times Doc came in and checked Colby. He had Anna leave the room while he changed the dressing. Anna pressed him for information... hope. "All we can do is wait and pray."

She did both but waiting was the hardest thing she'd ever done.

Slink and Tobias slipped in and out. As did others. Father left and returned. But she remained at Colby's side.

Sometime later, Father touched her shoulder. "Let me take you home."

"I can't leave him." If God granted nothing more than a moment more of his life, if he came to for even a fleeting moment, she intended to be there to tell him of her feelings.

"You should rest."

"I will when he's better. Would you mind putting Dorrie to bed?"

"I'm sure we can manage." He hesitated, sighed and headed for the door then paused.

She knew he hoped she would change her mind. She couldn't. "I'll be fine. Doc is here. His friends come in continually."

Finally he left.

She glanced around, realized there were no others in the room at the moment and rose to move closer to Colby. She touched his cheek, felt it only normally warm. Thank God. Infection was the worst thing to deal with. She curled her finger and ran it along his face, smiling at the way his whiskers rasped beneath her touch. Amazed at her boldness, she trailed a cautious fingertip across his lips, remembering with a mixture of pleasure and embarrassment how she had responded to his good-bye kiss, though she regretted it not a bit. It might end up being their last as well as their first kiss.

"Colby," she whispered. "Don't die on me. Give me another chance."

Chapter Seventeen

His lips tickled, jerking him from a pleasant nothingness. At first he resented it. He'd been floating like a bit of dandelion fuzz—effortless, bodiless. But a voice called his name, pulling him back…to a body that felt as if he'd been pinned to a barn door with a pitchfork.

"Colby." His name whispered past his pain. The voice was familiar, promising things he had never known.

His floating was filled with soft clouds. He struggled to break through to clear sky.

"Colby."

He knew the voice. It made him want to smile. It filled him with determination to fight through to the surface. Anna. He struggled to take the word from his thoughts to his voice. "Anna." It was nothing more than a croak. He tried again. "Anna." A little better.

He forced his eyes open, groaning as the light burned the back of his brain. Anna's face floated above him, smiling. He tried to smile back then darkness closed about him.

He lost count of how many times he flitted back and forth from darkness to the light of Anna's smile. If he'd been able to count. He tried. Got as far as two before he lost track.

Suddenly a thought blared through the fog of his brain.

Lew. He had to protect Anna and Dorrie from the man. He again fought through the mists. "Lew?"

Anna hovered over him. "He got killed trying to shoot the sheriff."

He sank back into blissful sleep.

The next time he opened his eyes, he knew the fog had departed. He was left with a deep fatigue and a body that hurt like fury. And Anna's sweet smile. "Hi," he croaked.

"Hi, yourself." She held a cup with a spout to his lips and he drank greedily.

"Am I going to live?"

She touched his forehead, pushed back his hair.

He closed his eyes and let his skin drink in the gesture.

"Do you want to?"

Did he want to spend years teaching Anna how much he loved her? Reveling in this contact between them? Enjoying his wonderful child? Before he could expect her to trust him, there were things he must explain. He managed to lift his arm and grasp her hand. "I want to tell you about Lew."

She pressed her fingertips to his mouth. "Later. When you're stronger."

He gladly left it to later as he let the pleasure of her touch fill his heart with hope and joy. He only wanted another chance to prove to her that she could trust her affections to him.

Daily he grew stronger. He was moved to the house Hugh had rented. He wished he could be closer to Anna but she came by every day, bringing him broth, or biscuits, insisting he eat. Once he was stronger, she brought Dorrie to visit.

As soon as Anna put Dorrie on her feet, the little gal raced for Colby, calling, "Da-da, Da-da," as if she thought the lost had been found.

"She missed you."

"I missed her." He reached for her, ignoring the pain in his side.

Anna noticed his grimace. "Take it easy. I'll lift her."

But he already had Dorrie on his lap and listened

carefully as she babbled away on some long, involved story. He nodded and murmured, "That's right" and "Yup" at what he hoped were appropriate times.

As Dorrie entertained him, Anna prepared tea. She'd brought cookies and the three of them sat and enjoyed the afternoon.

Eventually Dorrie scrambled down to explore the empty crate Hugh had pushed into the corner.

"To think I might have never been able to enjoy this."

"You might have died." She squeezed his hand. Her eyes glistened with tears.

His heart leaped with hope.

"I'm awfully glad you didn't."

"There is something I have to tell you."

She shook her head. "It's not necessary."

"I don't want any more secrets between us."

She considered him a moment, her expression seeming to offer hope.

It gave him courage to tell her. "Lew thought I knew where stolen money was hidden."

She nodded.

He hardly dared believe that she didn't wonder if he had a hand in getting the nonexistent stolen funds. "I didn't because there wasn't any." He told of Harv's method of control.

She only nodded. "He was an evil man."

Once started, he couldn't seem to stop. He told why he kept running from bad to worse. "I didn't think I could be what you needed. I didn't know if I could protect you." He still didn't know if he could or if anything he had to offer was about the same value as the dust on his boots. But he intended to stay and see this through.

She smiled gently and folded her hands over his. "You protected me and Dorrie by taking a bullet for us. I hope you never again feel you need to prove your ability to take care of us in such a way. But it isn't your protection I really want. It's you—here forever."

He stared, uncertain he'd heard her correctly. "Me?"

"Is that so surprising? Haven't we belonged together since that first day we met?"

"It's all I've ever wanted. There's a part of my life that is always silent when I'm away from you. I love you."

She tipped her face to him. "I love you, too. And even more, I trust you. Can you ever forgive me for not?"

He chuckled. "You had every reason to doubt me. I wondered about myself many times. But no more. Your love has brought me home and with God's help I will be the kind of man both you and Dorrie need."

"You are exactly what we need. No proof necessary." She leaned closer, her look intent on his mouth.

He could not ignore her silent invitation to a kiss and he captured her lips with all the hunger and love of the years they had been apart.

A little later, after many kisses, he tipped her face upward to smile into her welcome. "Will you marry me?"

She blinked. Her eyes darkened and she shot straight up, putting a chilling distance between them.

He watched worry and confusion flood her face. He ached to erase it with a kiss, but she turned to look out the window.

"What about Alex and Father? Who will take care of them?"

"Anna, come back here."

She hesitated then returned to stare at him with dark, bottomless eyes.

He pulled her close. "Let's trust God to provide an answer." He kissed her forehead, her cheeks and then her lips, trying to drive away the worry that had replaced her joy.

"I have promised to trust God through good and bad." Her words did not sound full of hope.

He prayed she wasn't looking for a way to refuse him.

* * *

She loved him. She wanted to marry him. But Alex and Father couldn't manage by themselves. She owed it to Rose to take care of them. As she tended her chores, her mind whirled until she felt like a top on a wild ride across a tabletop heading in a crazy path toward the edge and disaster.

"Father, I'm going over to the church."

Dorrie slept, Alex lay in bed reading.

She crossed the yard and stepped into the interior of the church. The slanting rays of sunlight coming through the west windows drew long shadows across the floor and up the east wall. The place smelled clean. The scent of new wood was still discernable. Her gaze lingered on the pew where Colby often sat to play his mouth organ. She missed seeing him there, sharing their love of music.

If she married Colby they could enjoy making music together every evening for the rest of their lives. Her heart jumped with joy and anticipation. She pressed her hand to her chest as if she would control the emotion.

If?

Had she already decided marriage wasn't possible?

She sank to the front pew and stared at the cross. Marred by the fire, yet a thing of beauty. Many had expressed delight with how Colby and his friends had salvaged it. Even Mrs. Percy had sidled up to Anna and murmured, "I kind of thought they were doing something special like this." Anna had smiled and nodded. But she recalled the suspicions the woman had voiced.

Was she like Mrs. Percy? Mistrustful unless the evidence was thrust in her face?

Anna lowered her head to her upturned palms. *Oh, God, you know my heart. How I love Colby and want to spend the rest of my life with him. And yet I know I must look after Alex and Father.*

Trust God. The words filled her mind.

She wanted to, but she'd never known trusting to be so hard. For a long time she sat with her head bowed as she fought an inner battle. *Whatever You will. I submit to You, oh, my Father.*

Unless God provided a solution, her duty was to stay with Father and Alex. She didn't expect Colby would understand her decision.

She slowly rose, and with heavy heart and leaden feet, made her way home.

The next day she moved about slowly, her heart weighted with her decision.

Father, bless his heart, never seemed to notice her moods. Except today. He lingered at the table after lunch and was still there when Anna returned from putting Dorrie down for her nap. "Anna, why are you so sad? Colby's on the mend. I thought you'd be overjoyed."

Yes, he was going to live but her joy in the fact had been diminished by knowing she could not share his life. Yet she made herself smile. "I'm so grateful. God is good." Trust was hard but she had set her mind to do so and she would.

"Then why do you look like you've lost all hope?"

She busied herself at the stove. Was she really so transparent? And if she trusted God, shouldn't she be able to find a bit of joy somewhere?

Father waited for her answer.

"I guess it's just reaction to all that's taken place."

She couldn't meet Father's eyes but was aware of his scrutiny.

"Has Colby been less than a gentleman?"

She gasped. "Oh, my, certainly not." Her hot cheeks at remembering their kisses likely gave Father reason to wonder if she was completely honest.

Father cleared his throat. "Anna, I am going to be very direct with you and I want an honest answer."

She stood in the middle of the kitchen, facing him, unable to move. When Father spoke like that, she knew she was about to deal with an unpleasant subject but she couldn't think of anything she should dread. It wasn't as though anyone had seen her and Colby kissing except Dorrie, and she thankfully couldn't report on their behavior. At least, she didn't think anyone had seen. Unless there were busybodies peeping in windows.

"Daughter, has Colby spoken of his intentions?"

Her breath whooshed out. "He's going to work at the feed mill once he's feeling strong enough. After that I don't know. He hasn't said." She hadn't asked. Her interests had been more immediate.

"I mean toward you."

"Me?"

"I'm aware you and Colby have always had a close relationship and I've watched it grow and flourish since his return. Does he intend to marry you?"

She stared. Father was being very fatherly all of a sudden. She wouldn't have expected he even noticed how much time she and Colby spent together. "He— I—"

"I would think a simple yes or no would suffice."

"He has asked me."

"Then why the long face?"

Tears stung her eyes, clogged her nose, filled her throat. She swallowed hard. Tried to push them back. "I can't marry him."

"Why ever not? Don't you love him?"

She nodded, too full of tears to speak.

Father studied her a moment then nodded solemnly. "I see."

She turned away, having no idea of what he saw.

"I've got a visit to tend to. I'll be back in a little while."

"Fine." She welcomed time to pull her emotions under control. *I trust God. He will only do what is best for me.*

Dorrie woke and Anna got her up. She should think of making some cookies but she couldn't find the energy. Must be because the house was so hot from the summer sun.

Or because her heart was so dull with sorrow she could barely find the energy to pack it around.

The back door opened. Father stepped aside to allow Grace Weaver to enter. Grace took one look at Anna and rushed over to hug her. "You look exhausted. Sit down and let me make tea for you…us."

Anna didn't have the energy to argue and allowed herself to be led to the table where she sank to a chair and managed to resist the urge to lay her head on her arms and have a good hard cry.

As the kettle boiled, Grace put cookies on a tray.

Cookies? Anna had meant to bake some but it hadn't happened. Grace must have brought them.

Father sat across from Anna and in a few minutes the three of them huddled around the table with full teacups before them.

Father cleared his throat.

Anna wondered what announcement he intended to make that required Grace's presence.

"Anna," he began. "You need to follow your heart."

She nodded, unsure what he meant. Part of her heart wanted to stay here and look after Father and Alex. She loved them. She knew Rose would want her to. A much larger portion of her heart belonged forever and always with Colby.

Grace reached for Anna's hands. "I know you feel your duty is to Alex and your father but I don't think you need to worry about either of them. I will take good care of them." There was no mistaking the soft pink color flooding up Grace's cheeks.

Anna stared, and then her mouth fell open as the impact of Grace's suggestion began to make sense. She returned her jaw to a closed position. "You mean you and Father…"

Grace grinned. "We love each other."

Father nodded. "I intend to marry her. With approval from you and Alex."

Approval? He didn't need it from her. "When? How?" She shook her head. "I can't believe it."

"We've been very discreet."

"I'm delighted." Anna laughed.

"You should be. You are now free to follow your own desires." Grace smiled gently.

Father nodded. "It's time for you to start your own life."

She looked from one to the other then giggled. "How long do you think it will take to plan a wedding?"

"Can we make that two? And I don't care about anything fussy." Grace looked terribly pleased.

"Nor I."

They grinned at each other. Father reached for both their hands.

Anna bolted to her feet. "I have something to take care of."

"Run along, dear. We'll watch Dorrie."

Within minutes Anna stood outside Hugh's house. Perhaps Colby had changed his mind. She smiled. He meant it when he said he loved her. And she trusted him.

Just as she trusted God and He had provided a way for her to let go of her current responsibilities. Even when she hadn't had the faith to ask for such a blessing.

Assured this was of God and propelled by her love, she pushed the door open and stepped inside.

Colby was resting in the chair.

"Colby?"

He blinked, his eyes widening with pleasure when he saw her.

"Let me tell you about how faithful our God is." She told him of Grace's assurance that Father and Alex would be well taken care of.

As she talked the sunshine came to Colby's eyes until they glowed.

She finished but he didn't speak. He just looked at her with such a look of joy that she felt tongue-tied. And yet he still didn't say anything.

"Have you changed your mind?"

"About what?" he croaked.

"About me." She couldn't look at him for fear she'd built a false dream.

He jumped to his feet, groaned with a reminder of his recent injuries. Laughing he pulled her to his arms. "I will never change my mind about you. And I'll spend the rest of my life proving how much I love you." He trailed a warm fingertip down her cheek to the center of her chin. "Anna, I love you. Will you marry me and make me the happiest man on earth?"

He waited, his gaze warm and eager.

She laughed, her heart so full she didn't know how to contain it. "I love you, Colby, and I will marry you."

"When?"

Her smile widened at his eagerness. "I think we need to discuss such things and make plans."

"Later." He lifted her chin with his finger, lowered his head slowly as if delighting in the anticipation, and then sweetly covered her lips with his.

"I knew it would take a miracle for you to leave your family. And we got it. Hallelujah. Let's thank God."

She gladly joined him in thanking their heavenly Father for providing a way for them to be together. And then they sat side by side, holding hands and talking.

She remembered his words about wanting a home. "Colby, I will provide you a home where you always feel welcome and cared for."

He hugged her and kissed her. "I know you will. And I promise to be a man you can trust at all times."

The sun slanted through the window and bathed them in golden light.

She bolted to her feet. "I forgot about Dorrie and supper." She leaned over and kissed him. "You have filled my thoughts to the exclusion of all else."

"Can't have that, now can we? Let me go with you."

Gladly she let him accompany her home.

Dorrie sat in her chair playing with a little yarn doll Anna had never seen before. She knew Grace brought it, probably made it herself. Pots boiled on the stove.

Grace grinned at them. "Wondered if you were ever coming back. I don't have to ask if you worked things out satisfactorily. Your faces say it all."

Anna and Colby grinned at each other, their hearts full of love.

Epilogue

One month later

Father and Grace stood together on one side of the pulpit. Colby and Anna on the other.

Dorrie wore a pretty pink dress Grace made for her. She looked like an angel in her father's arms.

Anna's dress was a deep rose fitted at the waist and wrists and falling to the floor in a gored skirt. She'd made the dress with Grace's assistance. It had turned out rather well, more thanks to Grace's patience than Anna's talent as a seamstress.

Colby had watched her work on it but saw her in it the first time a few minutes ago. His eyes had widened with pleasure that brought warmth to Anna's cheeks. How she loved this man. How she relished his expressions of love—his kisses, his compliments, his restrained hugs.

She shifted her gaze from Colby for fear her heart would burst from its moorings with joy.

Grace had chosen to make a tailored suit in dove-gray. "It will serve me well as the preacher's wife." Her ruffled blouse was of the same fabric as Anna's dress.

Father looked very handsome in his best black suit and white shirt.

Colby also wore a white shirt and black string tie. His grin threatened to split his face. He'd confessed he never stopped smiling. He said he fell asleep with a smile on his lips and woke the same way.

They'd talked almost round the clock as they made plans. Anna opened every corner of her heart to him, sharing her doubts, her misgivings, things long buried, long denied. She'd always had to be strong and in control.

When she told Colby that, he'd laughed. "You can be as strong as you want but never again do you have to carry your load alone. I'm here to share your responsibilities."

They kept the wedding plans simple. Just the four of them in a double ceremony and a few close friends—Grace's sister and family, Laura and Carl and their children, Hugh, and the men Colby had led to the Lord.

A friend of Father's had come to perform the ceremony.

"Dearly beloved, we are gathered here together…"

Anna had heard the words on hundreds of occasions but this time it was for her and Colby.

Father and Grace exchanged vows first and then stood by as Colby and Anna exchanged theirs.

Then the pastor announced the new Mr. and Mrs. Caldwell. Everyone clapped. He then announced Mr. and Mrs. Bloxham. Anna couldn't stop smiling as she accepted congratulations.

Later, as the celebrations came to an end, Father hugged Anna. "You have been such a help for so long. Now you can use your skills to build a home of your own. I'm so glad you and Colby are together."

Grace hugged her. "I will probably never live up to your reputation."

Anna laughed. Grace had already proven to be very capable and efficient. "I'm certain I won't be favorably compared to the efficient new Mrs. Caldwell. But I don't care." They shared a laugh. "I am so happy for you and Father."

She kissed Alex and warned him to be a good boy.

He grinned. "I have a job for the summer."

"You do? Why is this the first I've heard of it?"

"Father just gave his permission. I'm going to work for Mr. Ziegler." Colby joined them and Alex flexed an arm. "I'm going to build some real muscles working on a farm."

Colby squeezed Alex's shoulders. "You're going to grow into a fine man."

Then it was time to leave. Anna felt a twinge of regret as Colby lifted her into the waiting buggy and handed up Dorrie. She waved to everyone and gave a tremulous smile.

The buggy tipped as he climbed up beside her. "Why the sad look?"

"I'm just saying goodbye to the only life I've ever known." She shifted so she faced Colby squarely. "And I'm anticipating starting a new phase sharing my love with you and Dorrie."

Colby leaned over and kissed her gently. "We will build a home together. I can hardly wait." They drove through town, waving to everyone they saw. A few minutes later, Colby turned the buggy down a dusty trail to the prettiest little house in the whole county. They had decided to stay here for now and had spent many enjoyable hours preparing the house.

They didn't know what the future held. Maybe a move. Hopefully more children. But Anna was certain of their love for each other and God's faithfulness.

Colby set Dorrie on the ground and let her run ahead. He scooped Anna into his arms and held her there as he kissed her.

"You better put me down before you do damage to your injury."

But he carried her across the threshold of the house where he kissed her again. "Home sweet home."

She glanced around at the place they had worked on together to make livable. "It's simple but I like it."

He kissed her again. "I didn't mean the house. I meant our hearts."

She pulled his head closer and, just before their lips touched, murmured, "Our heart will always be at home with each other." From the first day they'd met, their love was meant to be. It had just taken them a very long time to be ready for it. But thanks to God's tender mercies and faithfulness to them they had a lifetime to enjoy it.

* * * * *

Dear Reader,

Welcome to the West where the heroes are big and bold (no matter what their physical size) and the heroines are small but mighty. As my father often said, "Good things come in small packages." Then he would pause and add, "So does dynamite." I was the shortest one in the family so the comment was usually directed at me. LOL. I often think I'd like to have been a woman living in the New West. Then I remember they didn't have central heat or running water, though, again my dad said, "We had running water. Son, run and get us a bucketful."

When I write these stories I wonder how to incorporate the facts about the harshness of life, then I remember it was normal for these people and didn't bear commenting on unless there was a vicious storm outside or a bear lingering in the outhouse. The people settling the West were hardy, stubborn and forward thinking. They have my admiration.

I hope you enjoy this story of two people who boldly faced their situation and through their growing faith overcame their personal odds. I pray you will be encouraged in your own faith walk.

I love to hear from readers. Contact me through

e-mail at linda@lindaford.org. Feel free to check on updates and bits about my research at my Web site www.lindaford.org.

God bless,

Linda Ford

QUESTIONS FOR DISCUSSION

1. Anna had witnessed her beloved stepmother dying. How did that affect her? Does it still affect her? How?

2. What did Anna and Colby share in the past? How was that undermined?

3. Why did Colby run from Anna's pain?

4. Anna has taken over running her father's home and being mother to two children. Is she trying to prove something by doing this?

5. Colby is afraid he will be like his father. In what ways is he or has he been similar? In what ways is he different?

6. Colby has come back. Why? Do you think he is right or wrong in doing so?

7. Anna sees activities at the church that make her wonder about what Colby is up to. Do you think she is wise in being cautious and even suspicious? Does she have a deeper reason than caution about the sort of men she sees?

8. Others see the drunks and down-and-out men visiting the church. Some of them are upset. What are their reasons?

9. Colby is determined to prove he's changed yet people see the company he keeps and wonder if he's changed. How does he reveal he truly is?

10. Anna's brother, Alex, changes because of Colby. How and why?

11. How does Colby prove that the most important thing in his life is the safety of Anna and Dorrie? Does Anna believe it?

12. Anna struggles with fear of loss. What helps her to overcome this? What would you have said to her to help her deal with this?

13. Do you think Colby is truly free from his past? What challenges do you foresee for him in the future?

14. Do you think Anna has matured enough to deal with the uncertainties of what lies ahead?

15. What spiritual lesson did they each learn?

One step into the living room and she froze
again, pan aloft.

A hulking shape stood in shadow just inside the
French doors leading out to the garden veranda.
This was not Popbottle Jones. This was a big,
bulky, dangerous-looking man. She raised the pan
higher.

"What do you want?"

"Annie?" He stepped into the light.

All the blood drained from Annie's face. Her
mouth went dry as saltines. "Sloan Hawkins?"

The man removed a pair of silver aviator sun-
glasses and hung them on the neck of his black
rock-and-roll T-shirt. He'd rolled the sleeves up,
baring muscular biceps. A pair of eyes too blue to
define narrowed, looking her over as though he
were a wolf and she a bunny rabbit.

Annie suppressed an annoying shiver.

It was Sloan, all right, though older and with more muscle. His nearly black hair was shorter now—no more bad-boy curl over the forehead—but bad boy screamed off him in waves just the same. He was devastatingly handsome, in a tough, rugged, manly kind of way. The years had been kind to Sloan Hawkins.

She really wanted to hate him, but she'd already wasted too much emotion on this outlaw. With God's help she'd learned to forgive. But she wasn't about to forget.

Will Sloan and Annie's faith be strong
enough to see them through
the pain of the past and allow them to open
their hearts to a possible future?
Find out in THE WEDDING GARDEN
by Linda Goodnight,
available May 2010 from Love Inspired.

Former bad boy Sloan Hawkins is back in
Redemption, Oklahoma, to help keep his aunt's
cherished garden thriving and to reconnect with the
girl he left behind, Annie Markham. But when he
discovers his secret child—and that single mother
Annie never stopped loving him—he's determined
that a wedding will take place in the garden
nurtured by faith and love.

Where healing flows...

Look for

The Wedding Garden
by Linda Goodnight

*Available May 2010
wherever you buy books.*

www.SteepleHill.com

Steeple
Hill®
LI87595

REQUEST YOUR FREE BOOKS!

2 FREE INSPIRATIONAL NOVELS
PLUS 2
FREE
MYSTERY GIFTS

Love Inspired.

HISTORICAL

INSPIRATIONAL HISTORICAL ROMANCE

YES! Please send me 2 FREE Love Inspired® Historical novels and my 2 FREE mystery gifts (gifts are worth about $10). After receiving them, if I don't wish to receive any more books, I can return the shipping statement marked "cancel". If I don't cancel, I will receive 4 brand-new novels every other month and be billed just $4.24 per book in the U.S. or $4.74 per book in Canada. That's a saving of over 20% off the cover price. It's quite a bargain! Shipping and handling is just 50¢ per book in the U.S. and 75¢ per book in Canada.* I understand that accepting the 2 free books and gifts places me under no obligation to buy anything. I can always return a shipment and cancel at any time. Even if I never buy another book, the two free books and gifts are mine to keep forever.

102 IDN E4LC   302 IDN E4LN

Name _____ (PLEASE PRINT) _____

Address _____ Apt. #

City _____ State/Prov. _____ Zip/Postal Code

Signature (if under 18, a parent or guardian must sign)

Mail to **Steeple Hill Reader Service:**
IN U.S.A.: P.O. Box 1867, Buffalo, NY 14240-1867
IN CANADA: P.O. Box 609, Fort Erie, Ontario L2A 5X3

Not valid for current subscribers to Love Inspired Historical books.

Want to try two free books from another series?
Call 1-800-873-8635 or visit www.morefreebooks.com.

* Terms and prices subject to change without notice. Prices do not include applicable taxes. Sales tax applicable in N.Y. Canadian residents will be charged applicable provincial taxes and GST. Offer not valid in Quebec. This offer is limited to one order per household. All orders subject to approval. Credit or debit balances in a customer's account(s) may be offset by any other outstanding balance owed by or to the customer. Please allow 4 to 6 weeks for delivery. Offer available while quantities last.

Your Privacy: Steeple Hill Books is committed to protecting your privacy. Our Privacy Policy is available online at www.SteepleHill.com or upon request from the Reader Service. From time to time we make our lists of customers available to reputable third parties who may have a product or service of interest to you. If you would prefer we not share your name and address, please check here. ☐

Help us get it right—We strive for accurate, respectful and relevant communications. To clarify or modify your communication preferences, visit us at www.ReaderService.com/consumerschoice.

LIH10

Love Inspired
HISTORICAL

INSPIRATIONAL HISTORICAL ROMANCE

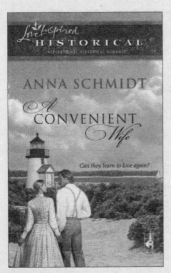

Widower Tyrone Justice has a simple plan—to convince schoolmistress Caroline Hudson to take in his children as wards. Instead, she requests a marriage of convenience! It makes sense, both for the children and for the love-wary couple. Yet, happiness lies within reach—if they'll take a chance on the unplanned gift of love.

Look for
A CONVENIENT *Wife*
by
ANNA SCHMIDT

Available May
wherever books are sold.

www.SteepleHill.com

Steeple
Hill®
LIH82835

HISTORICAL

TITLES AVAILABLE NEXT MONTH

Available May 11, 2010

A CONVENIENT WIFE
Anna Schmidt

LOVING BELLA
Charity House
Renee Ryan

LIHCNMBPA0410